The Quality of BLUE

by

Nat Burns

Bella
BOOKS

2012

Copyright © 2012 by Nat Burns

Bella Books, Inc.
P.O. Box 10543
Tallahassee, FL 32302

All rights reserved. No part of this book may be reproduced or transmitted in any form or by any means, electronic or mechanical, including photocopying, without permission in writing from the publisher.

Printed in the United States of America on acid-free paper
First published 2012

Editor: Katherine V. Forrest
Cover Designer: Judy Fellows

ISBN-13: 978-1-59493-263-2

PUBLISHER'S NOTE

The scanning, uploading, and distribution of this book via the Internet or via any other means without the permission of the publisher is illegal and punishable by law. Please purchase only authorized electronic editions, and do not participate in or encourage electronic piracy of copyrighted materials. Your support of the author's rights is appreciated.

Other Bella Books by Nat Burns

House of Cards

Two Weeks in August

Acknowledgments

I would like to thank my editor, Katherine V. Forrest, who said, very gently: "You have eighty pages in which nothing happens." I also wish to thank my Bella family for looking after me as I diligently make things happen in my books. And thank you, readers, for giving me a reason to make things happen.

I'd like to dedicate this book to all those who still truly believe love and passion do exist.

About The Author

Nat Burns grew up just outside Washington DC, in a Gaelic household, where she studied writing under the tutelage of the faerie-folk.

CHAPTER ONE

Beads. It had always been about the beads.

Ever since she was a little girl, River Tyler had been fascinated by any item that was small and round, but beads were a special pleasure. She had loved peering through the drilled center holes then rolling their glassy coolness endlessly between her tiny palms. Her bedroom had been dotted with bins of colorful beads and she would spend hours stringing and unstringing them, changing patterns and colors into never-ending variety.

Her mother, an extraordinary hippie philosopher, opined that loving the beads and continually restringing them was a useful exercise in humility. The perfect pattern always eluded River and no matter how many times she would line up a rank of beads, marbles or creek pebbles, they would roll at the first stirring, thereby proving how little real control the child had over them.

"I never should have taken you to Mardi Gras when you were little," her mother would remind her cheerfully. "By the time we returned home, you were covered with the strands of beads thrown during the parade. Made you into a little necklace junkie."

River knew differently; her fascination with beads had begun with Grandma Alice's pearl necklace.

Summers spent with Grandma had been a magical time, filled with fruit ices and the sweet scent of Mary's starched apron as River clung to her. Grandma's New England home was very different from River's rural Virginia home, with large, clean rooms that smelled of beeswax and grown-ups who always asked if she needed anything. There were also loud waves and sea spray, a pony named Pierre and a yard of manicured green grass that stretched off toward the ocean.

While there, the Tyler children's special visits with Grandma occurred three times each day. There were meals at the long, cloth-draped dining table, which were delicious, but the after-meal playtimes in the parlor with Grandma had been River's particular favorite. Perched on overstuffed sofas, River and her siblings would laugh together over silly books and make up grand stories of faraway places. Grandma Alice had quickly noted young River's interest in the long strand of plump, ivory pearls she wore each day and it became a habit for her to press the strand into River's hands during story time. She would tell River that she must take special care of them, and River would, lovingly caressing them until it was time for the children to go back into the care of Mary.

River had brought the memory of that enchanted, bead-comforted time with Grandma home with her each year and it had undeniably shaped her life.

Now, as her plane dipped west, River spied the line of islands extending well below mainland Florida and felt a surge of affection, remembering those pearls. She noted how much the ocean-framed keys resembled a haphazardly flung strand of beads. She tapped one finger against her chin as she professionally assessed the commercial appeal of such a necklace. It wouldn't do, she decided. Though a lovely panorama from her high vantage point, a necklace made from the too random tones of white sand, ice-blue water and the dull ebon of thick island greenery would never make it in the competitive jewelry market.

Leaning back, she closed her eyes and gripped the armrests with both hands as the huge aircraft veered into its final approach toward Miami International Airport. River truly hated flying. Each takeoff and landing was a small death to her nervously poised body, each disembarking a grateful ritual. She knew she needed to toughen up and get used to it but still found herself quietly humming Simon & Garfunkel songs for comfort as the landing gear lowered and the plane returned to earth.

The unfamiliar heat of southern Florida surrounded her as she stepped from the coolness of the red and white airliner onto the uninsulated jet bridge. Intense, sudden moisture sprouted on her forehead and above her lips. She blew a strand of damp, curling hair from her forehead as she strode into the huge airport terminal. It was positively frigid there by comparison and, stepping to one side, she paused to enjoy a blast of cool air from an interior vent. Stopping just then turned out to be a mistake as a large, rapidly moving body struck her from behind.

"Oh, gee, I'm sorry," said a tall, dark figure as she held River tightly to keep her from falling. "I was blinded by the sun coming through those blasted windows and didn't see you. Are you all right?"

Her voice was deep and mellow and an unexpected thrill raced through River upon hearing it. Surprised, she glanced up into a set of brilliant green eyes, the darkly tanned skin around them creased with worry as the woman studied her.

Regrouping herself, River straightened and adjusted the position of her carry-on bag, a self-conscious smile on her lips. "Yes, yes, I'm fine! Please...it's okay. I didn't even fall."

The woman relaxed her grip on River's arm and rose from a worried crouch, taking in a deep sigh of obvious relief. Her large white smile dazzled in the brightness of the airport. "Well, good. I'll continue on then. You have a pleasant day."

"You too," River called to the retreating form. She noted how the monotone dark blue suit and an almost military bearing stretched the woman's form into a lofty, striking figure. She carried a large brown valise with graceful ease.

"Powerful," River muttered to herself, as she touched the arm where the woman had grasped it.

She moved in the direction of the baggage carousel and spent a frustrating twenty minutes collecting one bag. The rest of her possessions were being shipped via a moving company to her new, as yet unseen, apartment on Petronia Street. The apartment, and Petronia Street, were still a good three hours' drive away, situated in the last of the chain of coral islands that made up the southernmost tip of Florida: Key West.

CHAPTER TWO

"Deidre, you have to listen to reason."

Patrice leaned back in the dark blue Queen Anne chair and lazily tapped cigarette ashes into a decorative dish. The small pellet of gray ash in its arid sea of blue seemed to cry out to Deidre for rescue.

"Reason? You've got to be joking," Deidre said as she pulled her gaze from the ashtray. "I've told you I can't get the prices I need from Anthony's group if I expect to make a profit. In addition, they don't have many good choices, their gemstones are cloudy, and the sales reps are too pushy. I can't even believe you are forcing me to do this."

Deidre sat across from Patrice on a brutally hard Federalist-styled sofa. She shifted in irritation, her back smarting with discomfort.

"Forcing you? Of course we are not forcing you." Patrice's voice was eel-like and spun with false gentility through the elegant room's frigid stillness. "It's a mere suggestion."

Deidre stood abruptly and walked to the living room windows. It was a futile endeavor because the heavy draperies covering that window were impenetrable. She suddenly felt an absurd sense of danger; of being trapped like a caged animal.

"Patrice," she began calmly as she turned to face the other woman. "When Simon and I decided to go into business together, he told me that I would run the business. He said he would be a silent financial partner only. I would not have agreed otherwise."

Patrice waved her cigarette nonchalantly, translucent smoke following her hand. "My son is not always the best at saying what he means. He dislikes confrontational situations and avoids them...sometimes to his own detriment." There was a heavier hint of Cuba in her voice this time.

Deidre sighed and resumed her seat across from Patrice. "Confrontation. So, in order to keep Designs by Deidre open, I have to use the supplier you recommend. And hire the manager from Virginia that Simon has chosen."

Patrice made a negating sound with her thin, deep-red lips. "We are only trying to make sure you have the best...from a business perspective. That's all."

Deidre eyed her doubtfully. "And if I refuse your suggestions?"

Patrice crushed her cigarette into the dish with one sharp yet lingering push. She looked askance at Deidre. "You are not a fool, Dee. You will do what is best for the business. We know this."

"I won't use Anthony, then. I need to be able to make my own business decisions about suppliers. I will train the manager you and Simon want—after all, she will be here tomorrow." Her lips twisted ruefully. "Not much I can do about it now."

Patrice stiffened visibly and her eyes narrowed into weighing slits. "This is true. I assure you she will be an asset to our business. Simon handpicked her."

Deidre lifted her bag from the end table and placed it into

her lap, clutching it for security. She was having that trapped feeling again. But she had to clarify one thing. "Patrice, I'm wondering…what do you see as my responsibilities with Designs by Deidre when the new manager takes over?"

Patrice cocked her head to one side. Her perfectly coiffed blond hair never moved but the pale skin of her neck, protruding from the mandarin collar of her silk shirt, folded into loose pleats. Her keen brown eyes studied Deidre with cold speculation. "Why, I'm sure I don't know. Perhaps you can enjoy more leisure time. All work and no play is not good for anyone."

Deidre studied Patrice in much the same speculative way. Here she was in this elegant home curved neatly into Foster's Bay, stocked with servants who did everything. Deidre wondered about Patrice's leisure time.

"And after all these months, I thought you had gotten to know me," she replied calmly. "Surely you realize that down time is not what I'm about. In fact, I believe the busier, the better. Designing jewelry is my life's work. It's what I do. I can't imagine not designing."

"Perhaps with River Tyler taking the lion's share of the mundane, you will have more time for designing new pieces." Her smile was wide but seemed brittle to Deidre. Deidre realized suddenly that Simon's mother had tired of her; that their interaction was at an end. She stood.

"Well, I can't say our visit has been entirely unpleasant," she said cautiously.

She completely understood the eggshell strewn path on which she walked. If Simon pulled his financial support from her fledgling business, she would be forced to close and go back to becoming part of another retail store's summer inventory. The bravado of denying their recommended supplier seemed foolhardy in hindsight. Especially when she realized that Patrice had not commented on it. Alarm bells jangled deep in Deidre's core.

Still, would she be able to look at herself in the mirror each morning if she caved in to Simon and Patrice's every whim?

"Thank you for inviting me out to the manor for tea. It was delicious. Few people know how to do a high tea anymore."

Patrice did not rise; instead she lit a new cigarette. "Thank you for coming, Dee. I'm sorry we couldn't work everything out to our mutual satisfaction."

Deidre tried to smile. "Well, that's what partnerships are all about…negotiation and compromise."

Patrice nodded and crossed her pantsuit clad legs as Deidre made her way to the front door. A grim manservant opened it for her and she stepped out into the brilliance of slanting afternoon sun, a stark contrast to the antiseptic coolness of the Minorca home. She took a deep breath of the sultry flower-scented air as she stepped to her car.

CHAPTER THREE

Larken Moore studiedly slowed her pace after almost knocking over the dynamically beautiful woman who had come to a halt in front of her in the terminal walkway. Though hurrying on alone, Larken still felt privately embarrassed, fully realizing how her overwhelming worry about Deidre had caused her to be uncharacteristically distracted and careless.

Deidre. Where was she?

Larken couldn't imagine what could be causing her absence. Usually she was as dependable as clockwork and her obsessive-compulsive tendencies meant that she was always on top of every aspect of Designs by Deidre. Something wasn't right. Larken, without even looking at her phone, speed-dialed Deidre again and once more the call went directly to voice mail.

"Damn!" Larken said, walking faster. Her thoughts drifted

to the treasure packed into the leather valise clasped in her hand; treasure meant for Deidre. A ridiculous urge tempted her—to gain comfort by opening the bag and running her hand through the round coolness of the beads. She wanted to heft their soothing weight and let the loose strands glide like quicksilver through her fingers. Yet intellectually she knew that today there could be no such comfort. Deidre appeared to be missing.

She stepped from the noisy coolness of the airport into the baking calm of the sprawling south central parking lot. She slid from her jacket and absently laid it across one forearm, enjoying the sun on her neck and back.

Though Larken was still young, just a few years shy of thirty, she had traveled extensively, thanks to her father's armed forces career. Pulling into another featureless military compound as a rebellious teen, Larken had looked out on the sparkling sun and water of southern Florida and knew she was home at last.

Her car, a sleek Mercury Cougar painted with the color and sheen of coal, welcomed from its parking space. As she settled herself into the vehicle, her thoughts perched on alternate possibilities concerning Deidre's whereabouts. Perhaps she was holed up enjoying a late afternoon siesta with her boyfriend, Evan, although this wasn't the norm, by any means. Was she running errands? In the past she had always answered her cell, no matter what her activity, even during some meetings.

Larken frowned. "Her battery has just run down," she muttered even as her mind envisioned the wealth of charging paraphernalia Dee carried with her most of the time.

At a stoplight on the airport expressway, Larken distracted herself by parting the zipper on the scuffed bag resting on the seat next to her. Glancing often at the light, she moved several folded garments aside and peered into the bag. The dusky gold of true amber winked at her from a plastic shroud. Amber, a rare resin from ancient pine trees, was beautiful and expensive. And this even in Africa, where uncommon, hand-fashioned beads often sold for negligible amounts. Although the amber was an unexpected expense, Larken wasn't worried. Deidre Collins trusted her because she knew Larken would help Designs by Deidre turn a tidy profit on the beads. There was money galore in South Florida if one knew the sources. And obviously Deidre could find them, if one considered her affiliation with Simon Minorca's mafia *cosca*.

Accelerating, the engine of the Cougar sounding its familiar purr, Larken thought of Minorca and her brow furrowed. She would never understand why Deidre felt pressured to avail herself of Minorca's money, thus exposing herself to *Cosa Nostra* treachery. She could have started off smaller, bought just a little inventory and hired less staff.

"Hell, I can string beads," Larken told the dashboard, with conviction.

Minorca, a thorn in Larken's side, was not the sort of man she wanted to be associated with and would avoid completely if the decision were left to her. Minorca called his arm of the family trade The Fellowship, and the scuttlebutt was that it was a crime syndicate that stretched from New Jersey to Key West.

And it was Minorca who had convinced Deidre to move her small business south from rural North Carolina and open the store in busier Key West. Though initially denying that he had a full, active partnership, Minorca now seemed to be ever-present, hovering at the fringes of the business. And Larken could tell Deidre was beginning to chafe under the farce of being in control while his Mafia money directed from the wings.

Minorca's money. Larken grimaced in the privacy of her car. Minorca's money had traveled to Africa with her and Larken had hated the feel of the cash in her hands as she paid the various bead brokers. Who knew from what pain and suffering that money had come? If there was justice in the world, that same money would now help those in need.

Larken gunned the engine as she turned onto Route 1, the highway that would take her home. Impatiently passing the blue and white crystal loveliness of Key Largo on her left, usually a welcome sight, she ignored it and fretted about her earlier decision to drive the chain of islands home when she could have hopped the same distance by shuttle plane in a matter of minutes.

Larken sighed, the exhaled breath expanding her lean breasts and stomach. There was nothing she could do about the situation with Deidre's business except make the best of it, take it one day at a time.

Deidre's absence, now, that was another thing altogether. Anxious and, if she admitted it, just a little afraid, Larken leaned forward, angrily punching off the air-conditioning and rolling down her window. Heat blasted her, immediately driving all cool air from the car's interior, a surrounding that better matched the foul mood she was fostering. She frowned and pressed the gas pedal harder. She needed to get home and find Dee.

CHAPTER FOUR

Driving along the tree-lined drive out of the Minorca estate and back to Route 1 and the twenty-minute ride back to West Key, Deidre relived the visit with Patrice as she dug her cell from her bag and fiddled with installing it in the car jack. She didn't quite understand why the elder Minorca monster felt she had to be so closely involved with her son's varied chain of retail shops. She grimaced at the dash. After all, they were all standard tourist-based businesses and surely required only whatever expertise Simon, even if he were somewhat backward, possessed. Or was there something more going on? It seemed that Patrice was the one who invariably called the plays while Simon ran them as quarterback. Deidre sighed deeply at the analogy. Sometimes having a high school football coach for a father bled over into all aspects of her life.

Suddenly, at the end of the Minorca driveway, just where it curved onto the access road to Route 1, a gardener appeared to her right pushing a wheelbarrow laden with branches. Deidre stood on her brake pedal and the car slid sideways, barely avoiding the man. Heart racing, she sat stunned as the man nodded to her and made his plodding way across the drive.

"Oh, good grief!" Deidre cried, one hand on her chest to still her racing heart. She forced herself to breathe slowly and deeply.

Deidre slowly straightened her car and pulled from the driveway. Movement behind her caught her attention and she glanced in the rearview mirror. To her surprise, two large men in well-tailored suits stood next to the wizened gardener and all three were watching her leave with unusual interest.

"Odd," Deidre muttered.

Within minutes she had gained the main highway. Relaxing finally, she switched on her MP3 player and a lively Beach Boys tune filled the car. She hummed along as she traveled the open road. She knew she should call Carter and check in, if only to find out if she had heard from Larken, but she felt a strong need to clear Patrice's dour energy from her mind first. Her thoughts drifted to Designs by Deidre, the new business she had set up in the downtown market section of Key West. Would it be successful? Jewelry was a luxury item and certainly not a necessity, so one never knew if such a venture would gain steam. Hopefully Simon's cadre of wealthy friends would bring them a steady string of customers.

She wondered about River Tyler and how the two of them would get along together. Deidre sincerely hoped that River wasn't like Simon's other bimbos but would be easygoing enough and less like the stuffed-shirt Minorca clan.

Traffic, as usual, had backed up on the causeway that sloped up and then descended onto West Key. Deidre reached and thumbed down the music volume as she prepared to join the queue of cars.

Only her car would not stop.

Mouth falling open in disbelief, Deidre stomped the brake repeatedly. Cold, abject fear washed across her in a paralyzing tide. Images filled her mind; she remembered the men watching her leave the Minorca compound and suddenly knew this failure of her braking mechanism was no accident. Reacting on instinct, she swerved to one side so she wouldn't ram into the cars in front of her.

The nose of her car plowed through the highway guardrail and as she soared through the air toward the reef of white coral below, time seemed to slow. Faces filled her mind; her boyfriend, Evan, her elderly parents, her dear friend Larken, her other employees—Carter, Sylvie, Len. What would happen to them now that they would be defenseless against the Minorcas?

CHAPTER FIVE

As River moved farther away from the airport, a new and beautiful Miami opened for her. Intense blue skies framed quiet, palm-fringed streets as the Atlantic Ocean worked its magic on land and sky. Following signs that led her across the north-south interstate, River easily found the busy causeway leading west to the remarkably well laid out tip of South Miami Beach.

Slotting the car into a place in the expansive beach parking lot, River stepped out into the bright day. She fingered her keys and then deliberately turned her back on the ocean. Bright, crisp skyscrapers towered on the inland side of the causeway, their windows flickering fireflies in the afternoon sun. Colorful, sleekly-shaped vehicles maneuvered along turnpikes and impatient horns sounded in the busy city atmosphere. Turning again, this time with her back to the city, River breathed in the heady scent of the ocean as her gaze frolicked.

The color blue, in its many varied shades, delighted her senses. The sapphire sky, adorned with wispy clouds, and the ocean itself, varying from turquoise near shore to deep cobalt in the distance, brightened by ever-swelling waves, inspired her. Slowly a necklace came to mind and she saw the piece vividly. Her hands twitched as she envisioned herself stringing the beads; blue lace agate—the darkest she could find—for the sky, green-banded turquoise for the shallows, and natural lapis for the deep sea. Yes. And unpolished brass spacer beads to represent the sand. She nodded to herself; as soon as she settled in and was set up at a worktable, she would make the vision a reality.

Bubbling with the excitement she always felt when a new jewelry design came to her, River strode confidently across the sand, tossing off her sandals and letting the waves wash across her bare feet. She stayed only a short time; the buffeting winds from the ocean, the blaring radios of the hard-core tanning crowd and the knowledge of the long trip ahead propelled her back toward the parking area.

She couldn't head out of town just yet; there was one more thing she had to see while still in Miami. Listening intently to the GPS system in the cell phone clutched in her hand, River followed the directions to get to the residential community of South Miami Beach and edged her car cautiously into northbound traffic.

While still in Virginia, studying art's influence on jewelry, she had read about the popular Art Deco-styled village that had been established on the long, narrow island east of the sprawling city of Miami and she was determined to see it. The structure of Art Deco was based on geometric and numerically even mathematical shapes, which was similar to the base of all good jewelry, and River had enjoyed learning about the heady possibilities of creativity within that style.

Then, without warning, she was upon it. Vibrant pinks, greens, and oranges besieged her, the colors caged within dramatic, geometric shapes on low, modular buildings. Sly structural curves adorned with imaginative fonts mingled within ornamental crevices, trumpeting risers and slashed circles in true Art Deco styling. Some of the buildings even bore the wide shoulders and eclectic modernistic angles of the art form. One entire retirement community had been renovated to preserve the sixties revival of the Art Deco Cubist form, an art form originally based on ancient Egyptian culture. Blending the old expertly with the new, the community of South Miami Beach did not disappoint River. Slowing and pulling to one side, she took several detailed photos of the more inspiring sights.

Passing the residential area, River drove into a more commercial district which hosted several neon-framed nightclubs as well as posh, elegantly detailed restaurants nestled within palm trees and pampas grasses. A huge, colorful mural loomed at a dead-end intersection and, slowing, she studied the artwork that made it seem as if the road continued on through a highly decorated arch painted on the side of a tall building.

She pulled to one side and quickly took a photo of the mural, sending it via phone to her mother in Virginia with the added text, *Landed safely and Art Deco rocks!* She grinned and pulled back into traffic. Following the curve of the true road, she soon crossed back over the causeway and found herself traveling south on Route 1. She sighed and turned on the radio, settling in for the long drive.

CHAPTER SIX

Worried beyond reason about Deidre, Larken decided to take the time and stop on Plantation Key for some advice from her friend Johosh Singer. Jo, who lived in a small house trailer on the bay side near Snake Creek, was one of the most well-connected people in South Florida and if anyone could find the answer to a problem, he could.

Though once a busy private investigator, when a stray bullet from a standoff shattered his lower leg, Jo had closed his business. These days he lived on an insurance settlement and occupied himself with keeping tabs on crime in the Keys and reporting information to the local law.

She spied him immediately as she rolled to a stop behind the blue truck parked in his gravel driveway. The blistering island heat never seemed to faze him and he spent most days out wandering his two acres of ocean-bordered brush or resting in the open-sided lean-to attached to his trailer. He grinned and waved from the shelter of this lean-to when he saw her car pull in. He rose and limped to greet her.

"Well, look at you!" he said evenly as he approached the open car door. "All dressed up with no place to go."

Larken eyed him with a raised eyebrow as she unfolded herself from the driver's seat. "And look at you, scruffy as ever," she retorted. She indicated his ragged denim shorts and sleeveless T-shirt.

Actually Jo looked well. He'd gained back the weight he'd lost on the pain medications and seemed to be perambulating well enough. His snapping brown eyes, peering from a classically rough-hewn Native American countenance, studied her keenly.

"Smart-ass. So how was Africa?"

"The usual. Hot. Dry. Where I was anyway. Nothing ever changes there. Not really."

Out of old habit, the two strode side by side out onto the mangrove marsh behind Johosh's house to look for manatees.

"Have they even been around?" she asked petulantly, her eyes scanning the crystal water at the mouth of Snake Creek.

Jo shrugged. "I heard one calling yesterday but it was gone by the time I got here."

The manatee were a special love for both of them; the two had met at a Save the Manatee rally in Florida City. The huge creatures, appropriately called sea cows, munched sea grasses in the shallow water just off the Keys and unfortunately shared that feeding ground with a large number of engine-propelled watercraft. Cuts to their broad backs from propeller blades had become so common that the scars had become a way of identifying specific manatees. Watercraft injury was the number one cause of manatee mortality in the entire state. And it wasn't just prop cuts, the crushing impact of the boat hull on the placid, unwary creatures killed almost as many.

Today the shallows were empty.

"They'll be back," Jo muttered with conviction.

"I know," Larken said, looking away restlessly.

"Listen, Jo, I need your help..." Larken began.

Jo sighed. "It's Minorca, right?"

"I dunno," Larken shrugged. "I'm going on pure hunch here but the fact is...Dee's gone."

"Gone?"

"Disappeared. No one I called has heard from her for almost two days now."

Jo whistled. "Two weekdays? Dee Collins?"

Larken nodded grimly.

Jo stared off into the distance, his long, dark hair bristling about his face in a persistent wind. "Has she been giving them any grief?" he asked quietly.

"She didn't mention anything last time we talked. Have you heard anything?"

Jo shook his head. "Nope, nothing along those lines. And I think I would have."

Larken studied Jo's face and Jo turned to look at her. Larken's heart clenched anew as she noted the sorrow and doubt lodged in his dark eyes.

Jo turned away and patted Larken companionably on the back. They walked toward the trailer in silence.

"Listen, you go see if you can find her and I will send out some feelers, see what I can find out," Jo said. "I'll call you later, as soon as I know something."

As Larken opened her car door, she glanced back toward the shallows once, just to make sure no manatees had arrived while they talked. She took their absence as a bad omen.

CHAPTER SEVEN

Walking to her new job through the congested downtown streets early the next morning, River was impressed by the casual charm of the small historic village of Key West. Though obviously catering to a busy tourist trade, the Old Town district still bore traces of the island's early days when most of the inhabitants worked too hard eking out a living from the surrounding sea. Cast-off parts of sailing vessels stood fast in sidewalk mounts as historic monuments and brightly painted statues of old sailors carved from wood decorated several public benches. Open-air markets offered fresh seafood, shells and sponges from the deep.

Coupled with the feeling of early island history was a definite tropical influence. Colorful banners fluttered in a fretful sea breeze above the heads of people who were speaking a street patois of many languages. Upbeat steel drum music sounded from a distance even this early in the day.

Following the map sent by Simon's assistant, River discovered that Designs by Deidre was located in the center of Old Town. Inserted discreetly between an oceanic museum and a store that specialized in airbrushed T-shirts, the front of the jewelry shop was a narrow panel of sparkling glass.

The shop was small, certainly smaller than she had expected, and the floor space was further diminished by two large glass jeweler's cases set at ninety-degree angles. There were several artfully arranged wall displays of inexpensive necklaces as well, all hanging in inverted triangles so their dangling pendants captured and shot the early morning sunlight.

Advertising posters of jewelry-clad models decorated the three walls between these displays. The fourth wall, the one opposite the door, bore a freshly painted, greatly enlarged version of the store logo—a huge yellow sun with Designs by Deidre written in red cursive letters across the blazing center.

Smiling at the pleasant overkill, River let the door swing shut behind her, causing the string of bells attached to the door latch to sound a light jingle. Immediately a small-statured, chubby figure stepped from behind a yellow-draped doorway leading to a back work area. River smiled and extended her hand.

"Hello, you must be Deidre."

"Oh no, please don't wish that on me!" said the woman in a heavy New York accent. "I got enough to do around here without taking over her stuff too." Her eyes narrowed as she studied the newcomer. "She expectin' you?"

River hesitated, stunned that this woman appeared to know nothing about her arrival. "I'm...I'm River Tyler, from Virginia. The new manager."

"Oh, yeah, she said something about that day before yesterday." With impulsive grace, she extended her hand. "I'm Carter Abrams. I'm just a stringer mainly but 'cause I'm older, I look after things while Larken and Deidre's off doing whatever."

"So she's not here?" Disappointment stained her voice.

"Nope. Left yesterday afternoon...said she had an errand.

We haven't seen her since. Damned weird too, if you're askin' me. I been here since she opened the place and I never seen her even come in late before…much less not even show."

Carter was a small, large-breasted woman with an unruly mass of auburn hair. Her features and mannerisms reminded River very much of rock idol Janis Joplin, though a much stockier version. Now, as Carter moved from behind the counter, River could see she was wearing an unusual working outfit: a long, flowing skirt and a billowing silk blouse, all in vibrant colors. Several decorative hair clips unsuccessfully tamed her wild hair.

"Well, it's good to meet you," River murmured. "I guess I'm more nervous than I thought I'd be."

"Pshaw, don't waste energy on that," Carter said. "Key West is the last place for someone to feel uptight. These people here are so easygoing, I worry sometimes they'll forget to breathe."

Chuckling at her own wit, she pulled River toward the curtained doorway.

"Come back and get settled. Dee should be in directly, though, like I was saying, her being MIA is really strange." Her voice lowered conspiratorially. "She's one of those Type A women who checks in two hundred times a day. I hope you're ready for that."

Looming large on the other side of the yellow curtain was a long, narrow workroom. White-draped tables, divided into work stations, filled the room. Haphazard stacks of clear, sectioned bead boxes covered the surfaces of the tables, their contents brilliant or subdued by turns. Spools of stringing materials stood sentinel in the middle of the tables and big bins of jewelry findings and spacer beads were scattered about.

River immediately felt at home.

"This is great," she said, walking to the closest table. "What an assortment."

"Yeah," Carter agreed modestly. "It's not too bad. Larken's been travelin' all over buying beads and she's finding some dynamite stones."

River's attention was drawn to the many boxes of beads and she began lifting them and perusing the contents, looking for just the right color combinations.

"I had this idea for a necklace..." she began, only to break off thoughtfully as she found a certain color she liked.

Carter waited politely, but as the silence lengthened, she grew impatient.

"Well?" she asked, amusement flavoring her tone. "Tell me! I'm dying of curiosity."

River laughed and shook her head, sloughing off reverie. "Sorry. It's just a piece about the relationship of ocean to beach to sky. You know, lots of blues and whites."

"Sounds beautiful," Carter replied. "Is it planned out or do you want some help?"

There was no answer as River lost herself in creating the piece, utilizing one of the many grooved beading boards.

Carter chuckled to herself and, grabbing up a pile of mail, settled herself at a nearby desk. It was mystifying, really, how designers could tune out the entire world as they put a piece together.

CHAPTER EIGHT

Almost two hours later, as if awakening from a long sleep, River blinked her eyes a few times and looked around the workroom. Her gaze fell on a girl of perhaps eighteen who was sitting at the table opposite her. The girl seemed to sense River's gaze and lifted widely spaced, dusky gray eyes to study her.

"Can we see it now?" the girl asked quietly, her round face filled with awe and enthusiasm.

River colored slightly but beckoned the girl over.

"Oh, my goodness," the girl exclaimed as she bent over the necklace. "Would you look at this? It's gorgeous!" One hand gestured impatiently toward Carter.

Carter sighed as she rose from her chair. "I'm not sure I want to look, Sylvie. It always makes me feel so inadequate."

Carter approached, the citrus scent of her perfume washing

across River. Together they studied the beads River had laid out in the curve of the board. The design differed somewhat from the original vision that had inspired River in Miami, but the concept was the same.

Nervously, River held her breath, wondering if the others would see what she had tried so hard to convey.

"I see it," said Carter quietly, as if reading River's thoughts.

The young girl, whom Carter had called Sylvie, turned to eye the older woman. "What do you mean?"

River's and Carter's eyes met briefly in special understanding.

"It's the ocean and the beach," explained Carter finally. "Can't you see it? Look again."

Sylvie leaned forward, wrinkling her pert, freckled nose in concentration.

Beginning at the center of the board, where all good necklaces start, was an oval disk made from iridescent blue and green paua shell. On each side of the shell disk stretched beads of dark blue—natural lapis and blue agate. These moved toward the faded blues of sapphires and aquamarines, then to the browns of picture jasper and the palest goldstone, with flecks of iridescence. The beads directly around the neck were six-millimeter aurora borealis Swarovski crystals with their sparkling pastel sheen. A small oval spacer made from pale blue lace agate beads separated each larger bead and gave it definition.

After another moment Sylvie's face brightened and she cooed softly. "Oh yeah, it's like the little beads are the tips of the waves. That shell is the deep bottom and the goldstone is the sand. The aurora borealis crystals up at the top must be the sky, right?"

She traced the nibbled tip of one fingernail along the beads. "That's remarkable," she said absently.

Carter smiled and shoved playfully at the young girl's shoulder. "I've told you, Sylvie, honey, jewelry has to have heart and soul. This must be what makes River here a master. She feels the pieces and can make them come alive by the materials she chooses and the way she lays them out. She's driven by beauty."

"May I string them?"

The request came from a back corner and, eyes widening, Carter turned to the elderly man who had spoken.

White-haired and with the weathered, deeply lined face of a true outdoorsman, he perched on a chair in the back corner, studying them with tightly squinted eyes. Compared with the other work areas in the room, the table before him was compulsively neat.

"Why, certainly, Len. That would be appreciated," Carter said. She lifted the bead board and walked reverently toward him.

"Do you think the silver or the gold clasp would be best?" he asked as she placed the tray on his table.

"You choose," she answered quietly.

"Gold, then," he decided with a firm shake of his head, "to bring out the flecks in this goldstone here."

"Good choice," Carter agreed as she moved back to the others. "Well, I suppose I should introduce everyone. This here is River Tyler. She's our new manager, come all the way from Virginia."

As Carter spoke, River noticed the woman's gaze kept drifting toward the elderly man who was patiently tying off the paua pendant onto thick tigertail wire.

"This little gal here, River, is Sylvie Baskins. She started just a few weeks ago but she makes a mean homemade pizza so we already consider her family. Ain't that right, hon?"

The younger girl laughed self-consciously. "I guess so, but I thought it was because I could tie off pearls faster than anyone else." She wiggled her fingers at River. "Small hands," she explained. Abruptly, she extended the right hand. "Nice to meet you, Miss Tyler, welcome aboard."

"River, Sylvie, and it's nice to meet you, too." River took the hand in hers and shook it warmly.

"And this man over here, still bravely putting a skeleton in your creation, is Len Paulus, our very own old man of the sea."

Len lifted his eyes from his work and nodded shyly in River's direction.

Carter laughed. "Now that's the Len I know. He's a man of few words."

Carter led River into the front of the store and briefed her on the cash register operation, the record books, and showed her where supplies were stored.

"I can't believe he actually asked to string your necklace," Carter muttered as she showed River the area under the counter where extra jeweler's pouches were stacked.

"Why is that so surprising?" River asked.

"Because he never talks. He was a commercial fisherman, by himself mostly, so I guess he got in the habit. Larken recommended him but I bet Len hasn't said a hundred words since they hired him." She paused for effect then added in a teasing vein. "I think he likes you."

Just as Carter closed the cabinet and stood, the bell on the shop door tinkled impatiently and a tall figure filled the doorway.

River raised her gaze and found it filled with the lean body of the woman who had crashed into her at the Miami airport. Instead of a business suit, today she was casually dressed in knee-length, rust-colored shorts and a bright T-shirt of mellow gold. Brown leather sandals adorned her wide feet.

Lifting her eyes to the woman's face, River realized anew how dynamically attractive she was, with glossy black hair cut blunt at her shoulders and slashing dark brows. Her cheekbones were broad and precise and slanted toward a strong, square jaw. Her lips, already curving into a smile of pleasure, were thick and sensual and covered big, straight teeth that were white in her tanned face.

The most arresting feature however, and the one that made her absolutely certain this was the same woman from the airport, was her wide-set, deep green eyes. They reminded River somehow of the paua shell pendant she had just chosen for the necklace, filled with rich swirls of green and blue color. These eyes now glowed softly as the woman regarded her.

"Well, hello," she said, her voice thick and luxuriant, reminding River ridiculously of the way fresh coffee smells after being just ground. "You do get around, don't you?"

CHAPTER NINE

Larken was delighted to see the platinum blonde from the airport again and to have the opportunity to study the woman at her leisure. She was beautiful, no doubt about it, but in a natural way, like an artless, adorable child. Her face bore no trace of cosmetics and Larken could see she had no need for such enhancement. Her wide, friendly mouth was naturally rosy and her pale lashes naturally thick and curled upward. Not that anyone would notice these things of course, unless she had her gaze fixed on them.

Even though Larken tried to draw her eyes from her face to study the woman's delicate body, she was compelled to meet that steady gaze just to reassure herself those eyes were real. Luminous in the face just above her uplifted nose, the eyes were almost frightening in their intensity. Larken thought of the cold fury of a hawk's eyes. Certainly such eyes could not exist in a human. Yet here they were, glowing in the midmorning sun of Key West.

The iris of each eye was a pale ice blue around the black aperture of the pupil. A ring of darker sapphire blue encircled this blue ice. The entire combination, coupled with the woman's long white hair, gave her an ethereal, frigid air. Larken felt as if, like thistledown, a harsh, hot gust of wind would blow this woman away.

"Larken? Do you two know one another?" Carter asked, looking from one to the other.

"Well, not really," Larken said quickly, trying hard to draw her attention away so she could focus on Carter. "We sort of bumped into each other at the airport in Miami, but we've not been formally introduced."

"Oh." Carter smiled. "Okay, let me take care of that. Larken, this is the gal Dee was telling us about, from Virginia, River Tyler. River, this is our buyer, Larken Moore."

River colored slightly but moved forward, extending her hand in greeting. "Nice to meet you finally, Larken. Carter has been talking about you quite a bit."

Larken, as she took River's cool hand in hers, was jolted as a lick of pure electricity washed across her body. Not since she was an adolescent in high school had she been so affected by the mere touch of another person.

Quickly, she dropped the hand and crossed to the glass counter, resting the valise she carried atop it.

"The pleasure is mine, Miss Tyler," she said politely, focusing her attention on the clasp of the bag that somehow kept eluding her fingers. "I wish now I'd realized who you were at the airport." *So I wouldn't have wasted so much time thinking about you,* she amended silently.

River, left standing by the door when Larken moved away so abruptly, glanced at her abandoned hand as if wondering what she had said or done to have caused such a negative reaction. Frowning, perplexed, she moved silently to stand behind the counter, making it a protective buffer between the two of them.

"So how was your trip?" Carter asked Larken.

Larken shrugged. "Uneventful. Have you heard from Dee yet?"

Carter sighed. "No, and I gotta tell you, I'm worried."

"That makes two of us. You are sure she didn't tell you where she was going?"

Carter shook her head, spreading her hands helplessly. "No. I did see her talking on her cell but she could have been talking to anyone."

"Well, it sure as hell wasn't me," Larken said petulantly.

River looked back and forth between the two. "I don't understand. Why are you so worried?"

Larken studied River, sure that anything she said about the Minorcas would go straight to Simon's ear as interesting pillow talk.

"It's just unusual for her to be out of touch," Larken said coolly as she pushed through into the back room, loudly greeting Len and Sylvie.

River followed her into the back. Larken stood at one table unloading packets of beads from her large leather bag.

"Check this out," she said as the others gathered around. "I found amber, and I think it's the real thing. I haven't tested the whole strand yet but four of them smelled real when I burned them a little inside."

Carter held the translucent strand of golden brown against the ceiling light. "They look good. Some of these are sold already. Mrs. Headley said she'd buy any pieces made from real amber, no matter the cost. She wears it for its healing properties, I believe. Better pack half of those up for her."

"Okay," Larken agreed pleasantly as she continued to unpack other beads. "And I have the usual; brass, wood, Ethiopian silver, and lots of hand-rolled and drilled glass. Just look at the color on these red ones."

A slow movement caught Larken's attention. Watching from the corner of her eye, she saw the new manager, River, move closer to examine the beads Sylvie held. As River studied the new beads, her left hand, the one nearest the table, slipped into one of the many open bins of inexpensive spacer beads that covered the table. Though her mind and gaze seemed focused on the new beads and Carter's reactions, her hand nevertheless plundered the bin of beads with sensuous abandon.

Larken sought her face. River's extraordinary eyes flickered to meet hers, the look questioning, but Larken saw no awareness that River realized what her hand was doing. The almost inaudible swish of the beads moving together as her hand parted them sounded loud in Larken's ears and sudden sweat sprouted on her forehead and chest. She dropped her gaze as her rate of breathing increased. *Damn!* she thought with furious exasperation. *What was it about this woman that unnerved her so?*

CHAPTER TEN

The walk home that afternoon was a tropical delight. The air was sultry now, almost too wet, too hot, but the natives of the island seemed to have gained a second wind with the cool promise of evening.

Many of the pedestrians she passed were undoubtedly tourists. They wore stylish clothing on their well-groomed bodies, the norm in busy metropolitan areas. Their shoes were the finest quality, their outfits impeccably coordinated, and their hair fresh from the stylist's scissors.

These were the ones who fascinated River; their sparkling diamonds and classic jewelry seemed to call to her. These were the women for whom she designed jewelry. The average cost of one of her pieces was several hundred dollars and River knew these polished people would pay thousands, even hundreds of thousands for the right piece of jewelry.

It had long been River's dream to open her own jewelry business. She had even chosen a name—Tyler's—a simple, no nonsense name that she hoped would rank right up there with other fashionable stores, such as Gucci's or Tiffany's.

Concentrating on the fine points of her future business, River almost stumbled over a young couple who were sitting on a curb embracing. Startled by their warning cry, she apologized and mentally shook herself. Glancing back at them, both less than twenty years of age, she felt a sudden ache in her chest. The way they gazed at one another, the special tenderness, these were the things missing from her life.

River was beginning to wonder seriously if she would ever have a relationship. The two she'd had thus far had turned out badly—the first because he truly didn't love her, proven by his infidelity, and the second because he loved her too much, at the expense of her freedom to think and act as an individual. Oh well, she mused as she strode onto Petronia Street, she was only twenty-two, and there was plenty of time to worry about love.

Inside her apartment, River dropped her woven handbag beside the door and flopped onto the sofa. Slanting sun from the window blanketed her face and upper body as she reviewed her day.

She liked the cozy smallness of this new Key West store and already felt at home in it. Dealing with sightseers had been fun. Few actual sales had passed through her hands during the day, but she felt confident that potential customers had been fostered. Some days that was all one could ask for.

An image of Larken Moore came to mind. What a strange encounter their meeting had been. Why had she seemed so cool? She pondered what offense she had committed to make Larken dislike her on sight. Larken had seemed so at ease with the other shop employees as they joked and conversed.

River turned her energies in a more productive direction. She eyed the many boxes that littered the carpeted floor of the apartment. Rising and fetching a cool glass of orange juice from the empty refrigerator—juice purchased impulsively from a gas station the day before—River studied the boxes with dismay. This was the first time she had moved into a home of her own and had absolutely no idea where to begin. Common sense dictated she start with the most needed items first so she moved into the small bathroom. A half-open box beckoned from the middle of the pale tile floor. Sighing and mentally rolling up her sleeves, she began unpacking in earnest.

Two hours later, River had emptied all but one crate of storable items and was feeling very proud of herself. She sat at the kitchen table and called home.

Unexpected tears filled her eyes as her mother's vibrant greeting sounded through the receiver.

"Mom? I just unpacked so I guess I'm all settled in."

"Yay, that's my girl! Are you okay? How's Florida suiting you?"

River smiled at her mother's enthusiasm, remembering anew how support and encouragement were so much a part of Margaret Tyler's nature. Her mother, named Kippy by her friends, never had a harsh word to say to or about anyone. Over the years, if someone crossed or wronged her, Kippy would ignore it, successfully soothing the defensive anger of her husband and six children by talk of divine karma and nature righting all wrongs.

"Hot, but nice. I think I'll like it here. You were right." River told about her first day at work, describing the shop, the village downtown, and the new people she would be working with.

And, as usual, her mother zeroed in on what was currently troubling her.

"What's wrong between you and the buyer lady?"

River sighed and lifted her eyes to the ceiling as she twisted the telephone cord in one hand. "Nothing really. She just doesn't seem to like me is all. How do you always know?"

"I know you, sweetie. Besides, your voice dropped when you spoke her name. Why do you think she doesn't like you?"

"Mmmm, well, she didn't have a lot to say when she met me. I mean, she did at first but when she shook my hand she pulled away. You know what I mean?"

"Maybe she's just shy with new people. Try not to be over-friendly and make her more nervous. Be pleasant but reserved until she gets used to you."

River mulled over this new guidance. "You know, you might have something there. Larken *was* nice to everyone else. There's no other reason I can think of that would make her want to single me out."

"Just be your usual charming self, dear, be sensitive to her feelings and you'll be fine," her mother advised.

River spent the next few minutes inquiring after her five brothers and sisters. Brother Moss had broken up with girlfriend Casey again, sister Tide had aced her science exam, brother Hickory had been called to the principal's office for his part in hiding the school team's basketballs, sister Sky had won yet another trophy in a karate competition, and baby brother Helios was up to his usual second-grade devilment at school.

"And Dad?" River asked finally.

"The usual. He brought me two bushels of green beans yesterday and I've been canning all morning. He finally finished that software job yesterday. And he's already sent it over to the university so they could try it out."

"Cool! Tell him how glad I am for him."

Vetoing the offer of talking to other family members, River sent her love to all and signed off, suffused with an intense longing for home.

CHAPTER ELEVEN

As she meandered through the outskirts of Old Town toward her home on Greene Street, Larken passed street performers who were heading out to set up for their money-making acts later that evening. Each day at dusk, tourists crowded Mallory Pier to catch one of the world famous Key West sunsets and the street performers during this time had become legendary. Many of the performers knew Larken and waved or called to her as they passed by on their way to the pier. Larken returned the greeting absently as she walked home slowly savoring the slanting sun and the sea breezes brushing her face. Larken was relieved to be back on the island but the worry she harbored about Deidre was really taxing her usual good spirits.

Walking around the perimeter of her home, Larken did her habitual check of windows and doors, and picked up wind-blown debris that littered the yard. Clyde and Ethel Baxter, owners of the villa, were absent much of the year and offered free rent as long as Larken took care of the property for them. She cheerfully obliged, actually enjoying the maintenance on the narrow grounds that led to the sea and the elegant, spacious rooms below hers.

Entering her balcony apartment, on the second floor of the typical Spanish-style villa, she tossed aside her valise, and lowered the temp on the air-conditioner. She dialed Deidre yet again as she poured cool water into a glass. There was no answer and now the mailbox was full, no doubt with Larken's worry-filled messages. Larken grimaced and pondered a drive out to Dee's south side home. In fact, she should have already done so.

Feeling the need for the exercise, if for no other reason than to loosen the tension knotting her neck and shoulders, Larken opened the garage and rolled her modified Schwinn cruiser out onto the cement driveway. She chose the cruiser over her faster, more streamlined roadster because she knew she was going to scour the island for Dee and needed a dependable ride that could handle any conditions she encountered.

A half hour later, sweaty and covered in sea foam from the coastal drive, she sat perplexed in front of Deidre's small cottage on South Loop, phone in hand. The place was deserted and a real and urgent sense of panic took root and began to grow within her. Evan. Larken needed to find Evan; he should be able to tell her something.

Her cell rang as she prepared to tuck it into its holster. Eyeing the screen, she was relieved to see Johosh's name.

"Are you sitting down?" Jo asked without preamble.

Larken fell back onto the seat of the bike, dread consuming her. "What is it?" she whispered.

"She's dead. Car accident on the causeway." Jo's voice was tight.

"Oh God, no," Larken moaned. "When?"

"Tuesday afternoon. I'm so sorry, Lar, I really am. I know what a good friend she was to you."

Larken fought back tears and for a long time couldn't say anything. "How?" she asked after a few moments.

"You won't like this. Looks like her brakes failed. She went over the rail into the drink to miss plowing into traffic." Wind buffeted his phone as he spoke but Larken understood clearly what he was saying.

"But didn't you once tell me..." she began, anger growing in her.

"Yep, just like Stevie Anderson."

Larken ground her teeth together. Stevie Anderson had been an informer for the Dade County Police Department and had worked with Jo on several cases concerning The Fellowship and Simon Minorca in particular. His brakes had failed just off Key Largo, sending him over the bridge into the water. Even though Jo had pushed for an investigation, the case had gotten bogged down with no one able to prove foul play. Jo knew though. And now Larken knew with certainty that Dee had somehow gotten crossways with the Minorca family and had paid the ultimate price.

Larken suddenly knew what she had to do.

"Jo, I gotta go. I'll call you later."

Larken walked her bike around to the back side of Dee's home and propped it against the wall. She knew there had to be some proof somewhere that would nail Simon Minorca's ass to the wall. Larken would be damned if he was going to get away with this again.

Reaching above the door frame, she found the key she knew was there and quietly opened the door. Some gut instinct led her to pocket the key instead of replacing it. The dusk-darkened house was as quiet as a tomb and Larken moved just as quietly through it. She was hesitant to turn on the lights, just in case someone was watching the house, but there was just enough sunset to fill each of the rooms with a ruddy glow. Larken knew her way around the place as well; she had stayed with Dee when the Baxter villa was being treated for bugs.

Moving through the living room, she scanned each table quickly for any papers that Dee might have left laying about. Larken moved down the long hallway toward the bedrooms. She searched Dee's room first and discovered a small document-sized metal lockbox on the top shelf of her closet. Larken didn't know what was in there but she felt certain it was better in her hands than in anyone else's.

Carrying the box she moved into the guest bedroom and then onto the smaller bedroom that Dee had converted into an office. In the last of the fading light, Larken gathered together any papers that looked important, especially any pertaining to Designs by Deidre. Luckily Dee's computer was a laptop and Larken laid the papers she found across the keyboard and closed the top just as car headlights swept the room. Larken crouched to avoid being seen and unplugged the computer, wrapping the cord tightly around the entire laptop. When the headlights went out, she peered around the side of the blinds just as car doors slammed outside.

Moving like quicksilver, she raced through the house tucking the laptop and metal lockbox safely against her chest. Gaining the back door, she passed through silently just as the two dark-suited men began to pick the front lock.

CHAPTER TWELVE

"Thank you for coming," Evan said, shaking her hand. He was a tall, thin man with smooth *café au lait* skin but still reminded River somewhat of her bookish father.

"I am so, so sorry for your loss," River told him, tears pooling in her eyes. She blinked and one tear escaped and ran slowly down along her cheek. She caught the tear on the sleeve of her black dress as she crossed to the table holding the urn bearing Deidre Collins' ashes. It was next to a large photo of her, and River stared deeply into the sparkling brown eyes and could see that much laughter had resided there. Overall Deidre had been a lovely woman with short, tightly curled hair and, for this photo, she'd worn large African-styled earrings. Although slender, by the shape of her shoulders, her face was just round enough to be friendly and welcoming.

"I wish I had known you," River said, one finger tracing the bottom of the ornate picture frame.

"She was an incredible woman," Larken said to her left. "She was good to me."

"How did the two of you meet?" River asked, watching Larken with curiosity.

Larken smiled and River decided she liked that smile, very much. "I was working on a cruise ship as, of all things, a galley cook even though I can't cook a lick. It was a seasonal job too which meant I was laid off during the fall. That first fall I saw this ad in the *Key West Sun* seeking employees for a new jewelry store opening in the area. I thought, what the heck, applied, met Dee and she hired me." She laughed, the low sound almost a purr. "I guess she sensed my talent for landing the perfect item at the perfect price."

River spied Carter coming toward them just as a muted cacophony sounded from the door of the small chapel. A group of five well-dressed men entered the chapel as one unit.

Simon Minorca, in his forties, was a handsome man, there was no denying it. He was dressed in a beige linen suit, tailored, of course, and gleaming brown loafers. His shirt was dark lavender, his tie a deep purple. Sunlight, stealing in through the big stained-glass windows, caught the diamond ear stud in his left earlobe, a bright contrast against the darkness of his closely cropped beard. His eyes and hair were a deep brown sable color, the latter pulled back into a sleek ponytail at the nape of his neck.

"This is a travesty," he said as he approached Evan, with a heavily-accented voice that rang with sincerity. "How could such a beautiful person be taken from us?"

He pressed one palm reassuringly into Evan's shoulder as he shook his hand with the other. "We can't express our sorrow for this loss. My mother has taken to her bed with grief. She sends her love and sympathy during this horrible, horrible time."

Larken shifted uncomfortably and River glanced at her, amazed at the scowl that darkened her features.

"Larken—" she began only to be interrupted.

"Look, I gotta go," Larken said to Carter. "I need to be someplace else."

With that she pushed through River and Carter and made her way to the side door.

"Okay, Lar...see you..." Carter said to the retreating woman.

"Carter?" River said. "What was all that about?"

Carter studied River as if choosing her words carefully. "There's some bad blood between her and Simon. I'm not sure what it is but seems like when he comes around, she goes."

River nodded as if she understood but her mind was whirling with unanswered questions.

"River? Is that you?" Simon said next to her. "Gentlemen, this is the one I've been raving about, my lovely antebellum beauty." Although he addressed the four men with him, his eyes never left River and she felt sullied somehow by the way his eyes roved across her.

"Simon. How have you been? I'm sorry we have to meet again under such sad circumstances."

Simon had finally pulled his eyes from her and was looking at the photo of Deidre. "Yes, it is. I guess heaven really did need another angel."

Carter sighed. "She was such a wonderful person."

"Indeed," Simon agreed.

One of the men with Simon leaned close and muttered in his ear. Simon nodded then turned back to River. "So, my dear, you are settled in? Do you like the apartment? I worried it was small..."

"No, it's perfect," River replied quickly. "I can't thank you enough for providing me with this wonderful opportunity. I just wish I could have met Deidre and learned from her."

Simon nodded thoughtfully. "Ahh, *chica*, it is a sad thing. But the store is yours now and you will carry on her good work. I need to go now, duty calls, but you must let me know right away if you need anything at all, yes?"

River blushed as he took her hand and pressed his lips to it. His gaze smoldered which made her decidedly uncomfortable. He took Carter's hand in farewell before moving down the center aisle of the chapel, entourage following closely.

CHAPTER THIRTEEN

Larken's sharp eyes followed River's approach onto the pier and she sighed. River spotted her and smiled shyly. Her pristine beauty impacted Larken once again and she chafed as she realized she was helplessly returning the smile, even lifting one hand in a wave of welcome.

"Lordyjordie! Who is she?" Beebee asked as he gave a low whistle of appreciation. "Do you know her?" He eyed Larken mistrustfully.

Larken frowned and gave her friend an irritated glance.

Beebee, who made a good living interpreting the messages of the universe, returned the look with an eerie complacency. "Well?"

"She's the new woman, at Deidre's. Going to manage the store."

Beebee shook his head and studied the ground. "Man, am I

in the wrong business. I never get to meet the babes. How did you get to be so lucky?"

"I wouldn't call it luck," Larken replied uneasily. "She's already taken and besides, she's not my type."

"Then you must be dead," Beebee muttered as River paused before them.

"Hello, Larken," she said nervously. "It's good to see you again. I guess the saying 'it's a small world' is especially appropriate on an island."

Larken studied her with cool eyes. "Yes, it seems that way."

She was perplexed to discover that she was still physically affected by River's nearness. Her heart was racing.

"And this," she said quickly, "is Beebee Gaines, a friend of mine. Beebee, this is River Tyler, from Virginia."

"River. Now isn't that an unusual name," Beebee said, rising and extending his hand.

River chuckled as she took his hand. "You think that's bad? I have a baby brother named Helios, after a sun god."

"Creative parents?" Beebee asked, raising an eyebrow as he resumed his perch next to Larken on the pier's concrete fencing.

"Well, sort of. Personally, I think they never left the sixties behind. They're great people though, so whatever made them that way, it's okay by me."

Beebee nodded his understanding. "So, how does the island compare to home? Any regrets?"

"Not yet," she said, shrugging her slim shoulders. "I really love the sea wind that blows here all the time. I didn't get that at home; we lived in the middle of a pine forest."

She lifted her pert nose into the wind and the wind responded by caressing and shifting thin strands of her hair.

Larken studied River with definite unease. She was so lovely, even with her fantastic eyes closed. A sudden worry beset her. Would she be able to remain impassive to River's charms, when they would be working together in such a small store?

River turned suddenly and fixed Larken with those remarkable eyes and she saw they were lit with a child's excitement and wonder. In that moment, she found it hard to believe that

River was the ruthless vixen she knew her to be. Scowling in confusion, she turned her face away.

River saw Larken's scowl and her feelings were crushed anew. Damn the woman! What had she ever done to her? Miffed, she turned her attention to the swelling green-blue ocean. As promised, the sky above the water was darkening with vivid rainbow hues. The sun itself had deepened to a rich crimson as it prepared to kiss the western hemisphere goodnight.

"Pretty great, isn't it?" Beebee asked at her elbow. "Even if you hated crowds, this would be reason enough to stay. Hey, have you seen the action yet?"

"Action? What action?"

"Oh man, come on!" He took her hand and gently pulled her toward the lower end of the wide concrete embankment that covered the shore behind the pier. River looked back once with alarm but was reassured to see Larken following at a sedate pace.

Pausing at the outskirts of a large throng, Beebee sought the easiest access then pushed through the mass of people, River in tow. Excusing himself to strangers and greeting friends, Beebee soon had the three of them at the front of the crowd where they could better see the street performers as they worked.

Inhaling with shock, River narrowly missed bumping into a man who was swallowing a sword. She watched with wide eyes as the long blade slid into his esophagus with an audible snick. Flourishing grandly, he removed the sword and River shuddered when she saw movement deep within the tissues of his neck as he withdrew it. The young daredevil turned, smiled at her and offered the blade with a questioning glance. Laughing, River shook her head, gesturing the weapon away. The performer shrugged and slammed the sword into a tall basket and proceeded to insert a small dagger into the pierced septum of his nose.

Beebee directed her attention to a second man, a tall, thin Jamaican, who had just begun stuffing his elongated form into a two-foot square cube made from clear plastic. She watched with open-mouthed wonder as he, with much hitching and compression, wrapped himself into a small ball and drew his whole body, even his dreadlocked head into the cube. The crowd clapped and tossed money into the knitted cap he had left gaping to one side.

Over to their left, a third man was encouraging people from the crowd to walk on his back as he lay prone on a bed of broken glass. He deliberately chose large, beefy men to impress the spectators and finally one big fellow, urged on by cheering friends, came forward and flexed his muscles. With a mocking display of fear, the performer carefully laid stomach first onto the broken bottles and drinking glasses in his makeshift bed. Arms held by his friends, the large spectator stepped with wobbly form onto the waiting back and took a few steps before falling to one side. With much aplomb, the performer leapt to his feet and exposed his bare, glass-speckled stomach to the crowd. Brushing the hanging glass shards off into the bed he cheerfully caught the bills and coins they showered upon him.

"Hey, did you know I got my start here?" Beebee asked suddenly.

"Really? What do you do?"

They passed through a bottleneck and stepped into a quieter section of the embankment.

"I read Tarot cards, you know, told fortunes."

River studied Beebee with new eyes. "That's fantastic! My mother is real big into the cards and interprets them for friends. She doesn't get paid though."

Beebee laughed sheepishly as Larken's snigger sounded from behind them. "Yeah, well, occult law says that you're not really supposed to charge a fee but...hey, a man's gotta make a living and that's what I know how to do. Besides, I feel like I'm helping people, you know, keeping them on the right path."

"Oh, I'm not judging you," River said hastily. "I think it's great."

They paused at the line where ocean lapped against the high concrete embankment and watched as the burnt orange sun bathed in an ocean lit by many hues of darkness. The clouds above the sun lolled lazily upon drifts of orange, red, and several shades of turquoise blue.

Slowly, all around River, the people on the pier, spectators and performers alike, moved toward the embankment. A sound began, sporadic at first, but soon gaining momentum. It was the sound of hands coming together in slow applause for the beauty of nature. By the time the final curve of the crimson sun spun below the horizon in a pool of blood-color, the sound was a crescendo of applause and River found herself joining in, thanking nature for the show-stopping performance.

CHAPTER FOURTEEN

As the Mallory Square streetlights stuttered into brightness, River took a deep breath and prepared to make her way home. Before she could say her goodbyes, Beebee spoke.

"Larken and I usually go to Freda's about this time. Want to come along?"

"Freda's?"

"It's just a little music club. You'll enjoy it if you like progressive folk music. It's a nice place, nothing rowdy, I promise."

River's eyes flew uncertainly to Larken's face. Was she intruding on an established relationship? The woman's expression remained impassive, blank. Angered and made stubborn by her co-worker's attitude of studied indifference, River agreed and they walked inland.

Inviting lights decorated most of the businesses and River was surprised to see how many were still open to the nighttime crowd. Music blared from doorways as young and old alike milled in and out of the nightclubs along the sidewalk.

"Boy, this place really comes to life at night, doesn't it," murmured River, excited by the unfamiliar chaos. Food scents washed over her and she realized how hungry she had become since lunchtime.

"Does Freda's have food?" she asked Beebee, her stomach rumbling.

"Yeah, but it's not great," he answered, adding. "If you're hungry, you gotta try Oka's place. Now she has some good food. Come to think of it, I could use some chow myself. How 'bout you, Lar?"

Without waiting for an answer, Beebee changed their direction, leading them along a quieter side street and back onto a second crowded boulevard.

A block later they stopped before a street side diner with padded stools set directly into the concrete of the walk. Each of the nine stools bore customers and River was dismayed to see a kebab filled with chunks of meat being passed to a young man.

"Oh, hey, guys, I should tell you. I..." She cleared her throat. "I don't eat meat."

"It's okay," Larken said with something like reluctance in her voice. "I eat the noodle soup here. It's good. They make it with vegetable broth."

River nodded and they waited in silence. Within minutes, one stool was vacated and the two regulars insisted River take it. They stood protectively behind her.

The proprietor of the diner, who moved back and forth like a whirlwind, darting in and out of the harried employees, was a tiny Asian woman with a long black braid hanging down her doll-sized back. Spying River and her two shadows, she cried out happily and rushed to pat the hands River rested on the counter.

"Aiyee," she said, glancing at Larken and Beebee. "'Bout time bring new pretty woman see Serioka. What name, honey?"

River, with a surprised grin, told the woman her name.

"Yes, pretty woman, pretty name, same, same." She grinned widely, showing a wealth of golden teeth. "I be so pretty too, wouldn't say? Ahh?" She nudged River's shoulder and mimed playfully.

River smiled in confusion as the woman cackled gleefully. She glanced back to see Larken's reaction and caught an unguarded smile. Larken definitely had a nice smile. She paused to study Beebee's ash-blond, puppy-like handsomeness. Though acne scars pocked his full cheeks, his merry brown eyes made up for the slight flaw.

A seat emptied on her left and Beebee scrambled aboard, shouting his order to one of the workers. Larken, obviously used to Beebee's impetuous rudeness, leaned over River's shoulder and ordered two servings of noodle soup before warning Serioka, with teasing good humor, about the folly of teasing the customers.

The scent of Larken filled River's nostrils and the sudden heat of the body against her shoulder was compelling. She had a foolish urge to turn herself to the right so she could connect with this heat. Damping the desire, she took a deep breath and found this just as disturbing. Larken's scent was something she had smelled before, something she was actually familiar with, but her mind refused to function when the woman was this near.

Thankfully, three seats opened on her right and Larken slid onto the one next to her.

Sandalwood, she remembered suddenly. She smelled of sandalwood.

A large bowl of steaming noodles appeared before her on the counter. "Here," said Serioka, handing her a long paper-wrapped package, "try chopsticks. Make fun. Sauce too," she added, grinning wickedly and pushing over a bottle bearing Chinese glyphs.

A young man set a bowl of the soup in front of Larken, momentarily distracting her, but she did happen to turn and grasp River's hand just as she lifted the bottle.

"Don't even get this stuff on your hands," she said quietly, taking the bottle and placing it on the counter in front of them. "I'm not sure what's in it, but it is some kind of hot."

"No fun, Larken," Serioka chided. "Why take all fun from Oka? Let new girl try sauce."

Larken laughed and shook her finger at the woman. "You better get on away from here, you Chinese trickster, or I'm gonna come back there and show you what hot really is."

Serioka lifted both her tiny hands palm outward to show defeat, a sly smile on her wide, tan face. She leaned forward and patted Larken's cheek maternally. "You sweet girl, Larken. You call you need anyt'ing else. Hear Oka?"

After she left, River thanked Larken. "Do you think the chopsticks are okay?" she asked, watching the little woman hurry around behind the counter.

"Sure," Larken replied, "she just likes to play. The hot sauce is just a type of initiation, I suppose."

As Larken talked, River unwrapped her chopsticks and expertly swirled them around in the soup.

"Umm! Is this stuff good or what?" Beebee asked River, leaning toward her and chewing with boyish enthusiasm. "Hey, pass me some of that sauce over here, will you?"

River started to state a warning but she caught Larken's amused gaze and passed the bottle over with a shrug. "I hear it's hot," she said as he took it from her hand.

"Yeah, I've had it before. The trick is just to use it for flavor so you don't get bushwhacked by it."

Carefully he applied a few drops to the kebab he'd been eating. He blew on the chunks of meat and roasted vegetables to remove any of the lingering sauce then cautiously touched one with his tongue. He dropped the kebab immediately and reached for his water glass as the employees, including Serioka herself, crowded around to laugh at his red face.

"Where does that stuff come from, Oka?" he gasped. "You need to put a warning label on it."

"Hong Kong," Serioka replied with a chuckle. "Label there, too. You just got to learn read Chinese."

River enjoyed the sound of Larken's rich laughter, which began as a slow chuckle from deep inside and rolled out in a calm stream. She also admired her skill with chopsticks. Larken knew the correct way to eat noodle soup, by scooping the noodles to the lip of the bowl held right up to the mouth. The broth was sipped like tea from the bowl. Few people knew this and the fact Larken did greatly impressed River.

It seemed everything about Larken impressed River. Her dark good looks, her tall, tightly muscled body, the deep green of her eyes. She seemed intelligent, too, although she held her counsel, so it was hard to be sure what she was thinking. Drawing her gaze away, River realized she had been studying the other woman and that Larken was chafing under that perusal, her wide shoulders hunching forward, and her face taking on its characteristic scowl. She felt chagrined for having made Larken uncomfortable, especially after what her mother had advised about not being overly friendly.

CHAPTER FIFTEEN

Freda's Tavern was located just a few blocks south of Oka's diner. The heavy wooden door was nondescript, obviously catering to locals rather than advertising for the tourist trade.

Inside was just as sedate; a small dance floor, a polished wooden bar stretching across the back of the room, and dim, recessed lighting. A wide stage dominated the area behind the dance floor and the musicians on the stage captivated River's attention as soon as she entered the room. The four men setting up their instruments were handsome, blond, surfer-boy types except for one thin, dark-haired ascetic. He reminded her of photographs of Grigori Rasputin, the way he watched her with dark, penetrating eyes as she moved into the room and took a seat at a small table.

"So, what do you think?" Beebee asked, eyes studying her jovially. "It's a nice place, isn't it?"

"Yes, and it seems quiet too," River answered. "Those other clubs we passed were awfully loud."

"Well, they're goin' after the hard core vacationers. Freda's family has had this tavern a long time, since this was a fishing town even, and they haven't had to change to keep up with the times. Business stays steady by word of mouth."

A waitress approached their table with an easy smile, a riot of blond-streaked hair swept casually to one side and pinned off her neck. Her lips were very red and her blue eyes darkly emphasized.

"Beebee! Larken! Good to see you."

Her eyes swept across River with friendly curiosity. "And who's this pretty lady with you?"

"This is River Tyler, the new manager at Deidre's. She's from Virginia," Larken answered in an even tone.

"Well, welcome to the islands, sweetie. My name's Barb." She paused as if uncertain whether to speak "I gotta tell you, you have some fantastic coloring, I mean, I know a dozen women who would give a lot for that hair color if they could get it from a bottle. And those eyes... I have never seen eyes like yours."

River murmured her thanks but dipped her head shyly, clearly embarrassed, so Barb continued, changing the subject.

"Virginia, huh? I'm from Maine myself. Decided one day I just couldn't stand another cold, cold winter snuggled up to my cold, cold husband so I packed my bags and moved south."

"Yeah, Barb likes it hot," Beebee threw in good-naturedly with a comical leer.

Barb stuck out her tongue at him and took their drink order.

The tall, gaunt musician was watching River again and she turned her chair slightly so she could better observe as the band tuned its instruments. He smiled once, inclining his head in greeting. River, not sure how to react, dropped her gaze to her lap, afraid to encourage him. Neither Beebee nor Larken noticed her impromptu flirtation as they had embarked on an earnest discussion about planned renovations to Beebee's home.

The musician turned away then and spoke softly to the other band members who launched into a folksy version of the Bryan Adams ballad "Everything I Do." River was held entranced by the music, her eyes misting from the sheer loveliness of the lyrics.

Barb returned then and placed a beer before her. Laying one sisterly hand on River's shoulder in silent passage, she moved on to the next table. The touch, fleeting and simple as it was, brought a deep longing to the surface. River missed the noisy companionship of her family and old friends and the easy camaraderie of her mother and father. This was new territory she trod, alone with these two strangers, both of whom now seemed oblivious to her presence.

Blinking her eyes, she tried to dispel the homesickness and took a deep drink of beer. The icy brew, frothing in her mouth and traveling a sweet trail to her stomach, soon warmed her and made her feel better. Propping her chin in the heel of her hand, she fixed her eyes on the musicians.

Dancing couples had moved to the polished wooden floor and it was through this curtain of moving bodies that she received the inviting smiles of the dark-haired lead singer.

After a spattering of applause, the band moved on to a slow song originally performed by Lionel Ritchie and River found her mind wandering. She thought of the incredible sunset she had witnessed on Mallory Pier, seeing the vibrant colors again in her mind. She saw the sun, a fierce orange ball, somehow cool in its fiery being, and wondered what gemstone could possibly match that incredible richness of color.

Intrigued, her mind explored the rest of the piece she was envisioning. There would have to be deep reds, not coral, not jasper... What? She scrunched her brow in frustration. And blues, pale and base blues, easier because there was more selection. Then the yellow, a pure yellow, a rich yellow, not watered by white. Not topaz, too brown. Citrine was too brown as well. Maybe yellow quartzite. Harder to find, but possible...

Her musing was interrupted by Beebee who took her hand and pulled her onto the dance floor. He turned out to be a good dancer, energetic and silly, and she had a good time moving to the rhythmic reggae music the band had begun to play.

Larken was thinking about going home. Being this close to River when they were both so relaxed was disarming and Larken needed to be on guard when it came to her new co-worker.

To make matters worse, River was dressed for the heat in skimpy shorts and a loose, very short T-shirt that left her flat midriff bare. Watching her movements on the dance floor, Larken was dismayed by the attraction she felt for her. Turning away, she closed her eyes and gulped at her scotch.

The throbbing reggae music was no help either, the heavy bass vibrating throughout her body. Yes, she needed to go home and needed to fight the pull she felt for River. Her mind drifted to her most recent lover. Sherry's sensual loveliness, her golden blondeness was so different from River's pale silver coolness.

Sherry had been in the final throes of a rough divorce when Larken had met her at Dino's Subs where she worked behind the counter. And this was what they talked about. At first. The attraction had grown between both of them; swept them away, and Larken had broken her rule about avoiding involvement with straight women.

Sherry. Her touch like wings flowing across Larken's skin. And laughter, a way of life for her, never seriously considering the way Larken felt for her. And then one day she was gone. Back to her husband, lightly, easily, and obliviously carrying a large part of Larken's heart with her.

Larken would never make that mistake again. She knew this destined her to be alone and that was just fine. It was safer that way. Avoiding women she was attracted to had become a way of life. But then along comes this new girl, another straight girl, this River, whose every glance made Larken's skin heat like candle glow.

Yes, she needed to go home, no two ways about it.

The thought of leaving River alone with Beebee gave her pause. Not that Beebee was a bad sort, it wasn't that at all. Larken knew Beebee would never force a woman into anything, no matter how beautiful or how irresistible.

She opened her eyes and turned to watch the two of them dancing. Since Beebee was a good man, why did Larken feel uncomfortable leaving River with him? With mounting grief, Larken realized she was jealous. What if River said yes to Beebee? What if she went home with him to his cluttered tapestry-hung bedroom? Suppose he read her fortune in the cards as a type of foreplay, luring her with gentle words and gestures until she succumbed to his seduction and the two of them came together...

Vivid scenes gripped her, River's naked form writhing beneath someone, her bright eyes clouded with passion. A sudden erotic charge left Larken breathless and her heart skipped several beats as she imagined herself as the one with River, the one giving her such pleasure.

Downing the rest of her scotch in a sudden gulp, she slammed the heavy glass onto the tabletop, causing several heads to turn her way. She stared at the table as she shifted her tense body uncomfortably.

Not to mention how over Beebee's life would be when Minorca found out he was seeing River.

And still they danced.

Impatiently, she gestured to Barb, who came to her immediately, worried, no doubt, by her anger. She ordered another round of drinks and sat staring at the dancers until the drinks arrived.

Several songs later, Beebee and River returned to the table, filled with laughter. Beebee flopped into his seat.

"She can wear you out, Lar," he told Larken as he sucked in gulps of air. "I think she's too young for us."

"Probably is," Larken returned with ill humor.

Beebee and River exchanged worried glances.

"Everything all right?" Beebee asked, leaning across the table toward his friend. "Something happen?"

Larken realized she was making a fool of herself, so she mustered a smile. "I'm fine. Tired, I think. Still getting over my trip to Africa. And then Dee..."

"Oh, hey, right. I forgot. Sorry, Lar," Beebee said, slapping the heel of his palm to his forehead. "We can go anytime. I'm kinda pooped myself."

River nodded her agreement. "I probably should get home too. I worked all day then did a lot of unpacking. I need to rest."

Beebee watched her with amusement. "Yeah, like I believe you. You were a ball of fire on that dance floor."

River grinned sheepishly. "I do like to dance. It's part of what I do for exercise, just get up and wiggle until I'm exhausted."

Larken smiled but noticed River watching the band with unusual fascination and soon realized one of the band members had singled her out for his admiring glances. This angered her anew and she felt depression tear at her. She was not used to feeling this way. It was exhausting, this traveling up and down on a roller coaster of emotions. She found herself directing this anger toward River. Was she returning the man's gaze? Or was she watching all the musicians? Larken couldn't tell but her knowledge of River as Minorca's woman of the month prevented her from giving River the benefit of the doubt.

Impulsively, determined to break the fragile connection between River and the musician, she extended her hand to River.

"Come dance with me," she said, more sternly than was necessary.

River jerked back as if in alarm and seemed ready to refuse. Larken sensed her reluctance and nodded toward the dance floor. "It's just dancing."

Glancing around, River noticed many couples of the same gender enjoying themselves as they jostled to the music. She nodded then, nervously laying her fingers into Larken's hand.

Beebee cheered them on, warning Larken to conserve her energy.

They moved onto the dance floor to the beginning strains of "Cry On My Shoulder," a song by Bonnie Raitt, and Larken knew her impulsive move was a grave mistake. The song was a slow one and she was forced to take River into her arms.

Larken enjoyed the feel of River's slimness too much as they swayed together, their bodies a mere whisper apart. Anxiously, Larken backed off, putting a hand on each side where the narrowness of River's waist met the gentle curve of her hip. Warm, velvet flesh teased at her palms where it disappeared under the waistband of River's shorts. River lifted her arms and clasped one hand on each of Larken's shoulders.

The dance stretched on forever and Larken noticed how uncomfortable her tense stance was making River. Guilt stabbed at her. Why should River have to pay for her issues? She tried to catch the other woman's eye but River avoided her for a moment, then, as if she reconsidered, she lifted her face to Larken.

This was worse. Larken gasped slightly as she found herself melting into the cool blue of the younger woman's eyes. So much of her was suddenly and openly conveyed to Larken—her nervous fear, a sadness Larken couldn't fathom, and a sense of excitement, of pure little girl joy that made Larken feel giddy and young. She was knowing River in a way that frightened her, a way she certainly had not expected.

River continued to smile tremulously at her and Larken was smitten with a desire to kiss those blushing, curved lips. She wanted to inhale that warm breath and lay her cheek sensuously alongside the smoothness of River's. She wanted to feel her thick eyelashes as they fluttered against her face. Most of all, however, she wanted to lie naked with her in the hot Florida sun.

Mercifully, the song ended and they moved back to their table. Beebee had disappeared but Larken spotted him at the bar talking to an attractive woman.

The band chose that moment for an intermission, so Larken found herself alone with River with only low music to cover their silence.

Reluctantly she cleared her throat. "So, you're from Virginia. What part?"

River fiddled with the napkin beneath her drink. "You probably wouldn't know it. A place called Bryant. It's near the Evergreen Ski Resort but that's its only claim to fame. Mostly Bryant is pine thicket with a gas station and a mom-and-pop grocery in the midst of it."

Larken smiled. River had a funny way of expressing herself and it was unavoidably endearing.

"Why do you suppose your parents settled there?"

River eyed Larken, seeming surprised that she would be interested. "Oh, they were some of the original 'back to the land' clan. They came in and bought the land when it was inexpensive. Just between you and me though, I think they really planned on forming some sort of kibbutz there but it didn't work out. Not too many people can take life out in the middle of nowhere."

"So what did they do? Keep the land anyway?"

"Oh sure, land is land and it was cheap." She smiled. "They had kids instead, lots and lots of them. I have three brothers and two sisters."

Larken leaned forward. "Whoa! Six kids? You don't see many families that large these days." She felt dizzy suddenly and knew the scotch she'd gulped so quickly was working on her. "How did your parents feed all of you?"

River laughed. "Well, we farmed, grew a lot of our food. My dad also writes computer programs and Mom writes cookbooks, things they can do at home. I guess they're kind of escapist hermits."

Larken sighed and crossed her arms on the tabletop. "I think that's great. Sometimes I think I'd like to just disappear and live away from everyone."

River cocked her head to one side and studied her. "It can be lonely unless you have a big family. Do you have children? A husband?"

Larken was surprised by the question. "No, no one like that."

River watched Larken with a calm, penetrating gaze. How did someone get to be the age Larken was and not have someone significant? River thought of herself and those she'd been with. Maybe she understood.

Silence descended as they both glanced about the crowded, smoke-filled room. Realizing a fresh drink sat before her, River thanked Larken and took a small sip, but unable to bear the intensified air between them, excused herself and made her way to the ladies' room.

River studied herself in the mirror for a long time, dismayed by her flushed cheeks and sleepy eyes. The unusual drinking was taking its toll and she could tell it was time to go home.

As she left the ladies' room, she noticed that the dark-haired musician was sitting at the bar. He watched her walk by but she ignored him, no longer fascinated by his rawboned appearance.

Beebee had returned to the table and he and Larken were talking. River paused at the table and took a twenty from the slanted pocket of her shorts.

"Well, ladies and gentlemen, I'm all done in. Is this enough for my drinks?" She laid the bill on the table.

"I've got them covered," said Beebee gallantly. "Put your money away."

"Don't be silly," River told him with a firm smile. "I pay my own way."

"Are you sure you have to go?" he asked, laying one hand on her forearm. "Stay a little bit longer."

"No can do, Beebee. I just started a new job, remember?" She winked at Larken. "Gotta make nice nice for the crew."

She noted Larken's sudden frown but was too tired to pursue the reason for it at that moment. "I'm sure I'll see you again at the pier."

She leaned in and gave Beebee a big hug. "Thank you for a wonderful evening. And you, Miss Larken," she continued, "I'll see you tomorrow. I did have fun. Thank you."

"Let me walk you home," Beebee said rising.

She pushed him back into his seat. "Don't be silly. I'm only a few blocks away and I can certainly take care of myself."

Larken rose and leaned to finish her drink. "I'll walk you. I'm going too."

River felt irritation stir. Weren't they listening to her? Did they think she was a child?

"I think I'll go it alone, if you don't mind. Really. It's only a few blocks, over on Petronia. I'll be fine."

"You don't know the streets, they can be dangerous," Larken told her. "I'm going with you."

Her temper flared unexpectedly. "Like hell you are." She felt a pressing need to escape both of them. "I've had a nice time, but please, don't spoil it. Good night!"

"What's with her?" Beebee asked.

Larken shrugged. Watching her purposeful strides as she walked from the tavern, the unexpected beauty of River's anger struck Larken numb. How her icy eyes had flashed as her back stiffened and her lovely mouth tightened.

"Well, Beeb, it's been good," she told her friend as she laid bills on the table. "I'll see you later."

"Sure thing, Lar. Call me when the lumber comes in and we'll do the job on the studio."

Larken smiled. "Sure thing. You take care now and watch out for the ladies."

"Speaking of ladies, get that one's phone number for me. She's a real tiger. I like her."

Larken smiled tightly. "I'll see what I can do." Suddenly, from the corner of her eye, she saw the tall musician signal to the other band members then leave the tavern.

A bad feeling rumbled in the pit of her belly.

CHAPTER SIXTEEN

When she opened the door of the air-conditioned tavern River gasped as the hot night air rushed across her. Though steamy, it was a beautiful night, filled with sensuous wind from the ocean and lively music from the steel drums of the street players.

She took her time, meandering along Duval Street, pausing often to watch performers. Soon the brightness of the main thoroughfare was left behind and she was very glad when she spied the street sign noting the corner of Petronia Street.

"You'd best slow down now, little lady," a voice drawled from the darkness behind her. "It's still early yet."

Shocked, River turned and faced the deep shadows.

"Who's there," she stammered, heart beating with frantic haste. Facing this new, unfamiliar threat, she vastly regretted her foolhardiness in insisting she walk home alone.

"It's just me, darlin,' no need to be afraid."

The man stepped from the shadows then and she breathed a small sigh of relief. It was the band member, the one who looked like Rasputin. Surely he wouldn't hurt her, would he? After all, she could get him in trouble by reporting any misdeed to Freda's. Nevertheless, she watched him warily as he approached.

"I saw you in Freda's place and I gotta tell you, hon, you are a fine lookin' piece of womanhood."

"Thank you but look, I'm really tired and I'm just going to go home and sleep now," River replied, taking a deep breath and turning away. To her surprise he grasped her arm.

"Now, now, come on. I thought we could party just a bit. Look here what I got." He released her and pulled a plastic bag from his jeans pocket. "I got some fine Colombian jumping powder, straight off the boat today. I share, too, so what do you say?"

River shook her head and walked rapidly along Petronia. "No, go away, please."

Moving swiftly, he caught up with her and wrapped one strongly muscled arm around her arms and body.

"Look here, honey, I just can't take no for an answer."

Acting in terrified rage, River flailed her fists at his head and kicked him in the shin. He merely tightened his grip. His hot breath, smelling of old marijuana smoke, wafted across her face as he chuckled at her futile antics.

"Don't fight the player, baby. Just go along with me and we'll see the stars together."

He bent and laid his hot mouth on the nape of her neck, moving her hair aside with his thick, writhing tongue and moistening her skin.

A moan of disgust welled from deep within and she clawed blindly at his shoulder, all the while lifting her knees in an effort to wedge them between this man and her own body to lever herself away. New darkness descended in front of her eyes and a sudden fear of fainting stilled her momentarily.

A hot wind passed over River, stirring the fine hairs on her arms and with a sudden shift the musician jerked back. His hands loosened and River used the opportunity to try to pull away. His hands grabbed at her again, only to be snatched away a moment later.

Stumbling to the sidewalk, River cried out as she skinned her knees and palms. Pushing a mass of hair aside, an eerie scene met her eyes.

The musician stood on the dimly lit pavement of the deserted street. He was in a defensive posture, but favoring his left leg. His attacker had gone, or was hiding, and the musician looked about anxiously. Then, as River watched, a blur spun from the darkness and descended on the man. A guttural cry split the night and the musician's feet left the road and accompanied the rest of his body as it flew through the air. A thin, despairing wail sounded just before a bone-crunching thump met River's ears.

"You didn't tell him where you live, did you?"

The question sounded next to her ear but River felt too numb to respond.

"Answer me, damn it!" Larken said as she shook River roughly, pulling her to her feet. "Does he know where you live?"

Anger replaced River's numbness and she slapped Larken's gripping hands away. "Hell no, I'm not that stupid," she told her with an icy voice.

"Look, you were stupid enough to give him the come-on in the tavern, who knows what else you might do." Her angry voice grated on River's nerves.

"Oh, how dare you...you idiot! I only watched him because he was so unusual, he looks like..."

"Well?" Larken was watching her, face shadowed by the gleam from a nearby street light. "Looks like what?"

She turned her face away, suddenly embarrassed. "Rasputin, okay? He looked like Rasputin, you know, all weird and spooky."

"Oh, please," Larken grated, "give me a break. Let's get the hell out of here before he comes to and follows you home."

CHAPTER SEVENTEEN

The two hurried along Petronia in silence, finally reaching the lighted compound of River's apartment complex. It was a good thing Larken followed River to the door because her hands were shaking so badly she couldn't insert the key into the lock. Gently Larken took the key from her, unlocked the door and pulled her inside.

With economical movements Larken walked her to the sofa and pressed her down onto it. Entering the small kitchen area, she put the water kettle on to heat then began systematically searching through cabinets until she found tea. Then she moved toward River's small bedroom, clicking on the light and boldly striding inside.

River watched her with dull eyes, the reality of what could have happened to her finally settling in for a good long stay.

Her scraped hands smarted and she pressed them together gingerly.

Emerging finally, Larken lifted her easily with one arm and propelled her through the bedroom and into the bathroom. A cold shower was running and fine, icy spray billowed from the stall. Opening the door, Larken shoved her, without apology, into the cold water. A gasp tore from River as the water chilled her skin and soaked her clothing. Water sputtered into her face and she screamed in fury, both hands reaching to turn the faucet handles.

When she slammed aside the stall door, Larken was waiting, face grim. Angrily, River stepped out and into the large soft towel held for her. Larken swabbed her gently, hands squeezing at River's clothing until the fabric stopped dripping. Her caring, patient ministration proved too much and harsh sobs ripped from River's throat.

In an instant she was enfolded, towel and all, into Larken's embrace. Larken held her close, capable hands cradling the back of her head as she sobbed her delayed reaction into the cotton cloth covering the solid, gently rounded chest. Larken held her that way for a long time, until the piercing whistle of the boiling water kettle finally penetrated.

Reluctantly, swiping at her eyes, River pulled away. "You'd better see to that," she told Larken dully, her face turned away so she didn't have to meet her eyes.

"Put on some dry clothing," Larken told her quietly as she moved from the room.

River emerged a short time later dressed in her warmest robe, dark blue chenille. She held a towel in her bandaged hands, rubbing at her water-darkened hair with it.

Larken had prepared a tray and placed it on the kitchen table. She sat behind it, her face vacant as if her thoughts were far away. She noticed River finally, when she was almost at the table and set about pouring the tea. She had used the proper cups, wide, handleless and Japanese in design, and had known enough to mismatch the two.

With a grateful glance, River took the cup Larken handed her. She enfolded the cup in her two hands and savored its warmth for a long time before sipping.

Silence reigned but it was a comfortable one and River let it lengthen. She had no reserves left for idle chitchat and knew Larken had no need for it. Instead, she studied the glossy sheen of Larken's hair in the glow of the kitchen light. It reminded River of the lustrous coat of a river otter.

A quarter of an hour later, Larken silently, using gestures, offered more tea. She accepted a refill. A half hour later, the pot was empty and she lifted her eyes to the other woman.

"I...thank you. I'm glad you were here," she said finally, her soft tone floating in the silent kitchen.

Larken inclined her head, eyes dark and unreadable. With a sigh she rose. "Will you be all right?" she asked her. "Are you afraid?"

River thought about it and realized fear would be useless. The man did not know where she lived.

"No, I think I'll be fine. Thank you for staying. I know it's late."

Larken moved toward the door. "I wrote my telephone number on the pad next to your refrigerator," she said, her back to River. "If you get frightened or anything happens, you can call me. I live nearby and can get here quickly. Okay?"

Impulsively, River rushed forward and gave a quick hug to Larken's wide back. "Thank you again, really."

Larken stiffened and her voice was harsh and angry. "Yeah, well, next time do me a favor and be a little less stubborn when someone offers to see you home."

The door slapped securely shut and tears of shame and hurt filled River's eyes.

CHAPTER EIGHTEEN

Although River was early opening the store the next morning, she found the employee door's master lock already unlocked and Larken sorting beads at one of the long worktables. Larken acknowledged River's approach but quickly dropped her eyes back to the task.

River, undaunted by the coolness, moved through the room and placed her bag on a shelf just inside the portal. Pausing uncertainly, she moved to the cluttered lunch table to make herself a cup of tea. To her delight, the water was already hot. Larken's cup stood ready, tea bag lolling parched in the bottom, so River poured water into that cup as well as her own.

While the tea steeped, she rummaged through her bag, pulling out a plastic-wrapped parcel. She carefully carried the two full mugs and a plate to the table where Larken worked.

Placing the plate and cups down, she perched on the chair beside the other woman. Larken continued to ignore her so she helped herself to the food and sat back with a sigh to enjoy the peace of the moment.

Larken soon realized that she was sorting beads of fumed cobalt glass into a bin filled with small jade tubes and ground her teeth together in frustration. With a long, jagged breath of defeat, she sat back and lifted her own tea mug to her lips.

River was lovely today, dressed in a pale blue shirt and dark blue shorts. Her white-blond hair, drawn back into a ponytail, framed her face with wispy bangs to enhance the beauty of her blue eyes.

Larken drew her eyes away and they landed on the plate before her. Small flat cakes, pale brown in color, met her gaze.

"What's this?" she asked, leaning forward to study the unfamiliar foodstuff.

"Oat cakes. I hope you like them," River replied, her own half-eaten cake cradled delicately in her bandaged palm. Gingerly, Larken lifted one. Though they appeared fragile, the cake was surprisingly firm in her fingers. Hoping it was good, so she wouldn't have to lie, she took a bite. The cake was delicious. Rapidly, her tongue explored the flavors—honey, predominantly, but there were spices as well, something tasting like cherry, or root beer maybe.

"What *is* this?" she exclaimed joyfully.

River giggled and pulled one slim leg up into the chair, propping the sole of her foot on the seat. "Good, aren't they? Sometimes I think I could live on these alone."

"What's in them?"

"It's my mother's recipe. It's oats, honey, sassafras liqueur, and a honeydew melon liqueur." She giggled again. "Mind you don't get drunk."

Larken helped herself to another. "They're good enough, that's for sure. Hey, these aren't cooked either, are they?"

River shook her head. "My mom is famous for recipes you don't have to cook. These are sun dried."

They ate in silence, listening absently to the growing traffic sounds outside the shop. Then the plate was empty.

"Customers soon," Larken said, beginning to chafe at their comfortable companionship.

River, taking the hint, rose and arched her spine in a stretch. "I guess I'll get on that cabinet. I wanted to get it rearranged before business today. Now, because of my lazy breakfast, I'll have to scoot."

Larken forcibly drew her gaze from the body arched before her and focused on River's face. "Yeah. It was a good breakfast, thanks for sharing."

"Well, I owe you a lot for helping me out last night. I'm not sure I can ever repay...."

"Please, forget about it. I like to rescue damsels in distress, it boosts my self-esteem."

River returned the smile and moved toward the curtained doorway. Abruptly, she turned. "By the way, what was that thing you did last night, when you sent that guy flying? Was that a kick or was it just some type of major punch?"

Larken bent back to her work. "A kick. *Tae kwon do*, the way of foot and hand." She sensed River was still watching, waiting for more, so she gave her full attention and elaborated.

"I was a military brat and my dad was posted in several Asian countries. I just picked it up."

"Is it like karate? I have a sister who's really into karate."

"Yes, very similar."

She nodded, curiosity satisfied, and moved through the curtain into the front of the store.

Larken let out breath in a whoosh of relief, beads forgotten as she contemplated looking for a new job.

CHAPTER NINETEEN

Just about ten o'clock that morning Simon Minorca strode briskly into the shop. As usual, flunkies surrounded him. River couldn't remember ever seeing him by himself. His arrival changed the whole atmosphere of the store, from tranquility to nervous energy.

River, reaching into one of the glass cases to replace a bracelet she had shown a customer, rose hastily and watched his approach.

He spotted her immediately and rushed to her, his entourage politely moving through the few customers in the store.

"Ah, my River, my beauty, how *are* you today?" He leaned forward to press a kiss to each of her cheeks. The moisture lingered, making her want to scrub at both cheeks with her shoulders. "It is so good to see you again. How are things going?"

River gave Simon a tolerant smile then peered helplessly at the woman she had been talking with. The customer smiled her encouragement and mimed that she would return another time. A young couple who had been browsing also chose that moment to leave and River found herself alone with Simon and his men.

"Just fine. I think I am getting into the swing of the business. Thank you once again for suggesting me for this position."

Simon took her hand and pulled her from behind the counter. "I must confess, the move was a selfish one. I have a home here in the Keys, you see, and I am sure I will enjoy having you close to me."

Larken stepped through the curtain, Sylvie on her heels. They must have heard the commotion of Simon's entrance.

"Well, Larken, good to see you," Simon said, coolly stepping forward to shake Larken's hand. "How was your trip to the Dark Continent? You brought back many useful supplies, I presume?"

Larken inclined her head, eyes hostile and never leaving Simon's face. River saw her clenched jaw and wondered again at the animosity Larken harbored for this man. What had happened between them?

"Of course. If you'll step into the back, I'll be happy to show you precisely where your money went."

"Why, certainly," Simon answered, turning and giving his men murmured instruction.

After they quit the room, River moved close to Sylvie.

"What was *that* all about?" she whispered as she pretended to straighten the beading instruction books behind the counter.

Sylvie eyed Simon's guards warily before answering. "It's Simon's money that buys the beads. I think Larken resented Deidre taking Minorca on as a partner because of the money thing."

"Oh, so that's it," River breathed as she nodded her understanding.

Sometime later, the two emerged from the back and Simon's gaze found River once more.

"Isn't she a gemlike asset to this store, Larken? So lovely, so cool. She's like an ice princess from a fairy tale."

River blushed and murmured her gratitude for his flattery, ever mindful of Larken's cold gaze upon her.

Simon moved to the customer side of the glass cases and his eyes swept the jewelry River had arranged so carefully the day before.

"This is lovely," he cooed. "I like the way you used the big, colored glass marbles to highlight the work."

River shrugged. "They were in the back. I was glad to put them to use."

"And what is this? A new design already?" His darkly tanned hand splayed out across the glass directly above the ocean and sky necklace Len Paulus had strung the day before. "I must have it for my mother. It will remind her of the sea and," he lifted his dark eyes to meet hers, "it will remind her of you, as well."

River was speechless. She felt impaled by his steady stare and at a loss as to know what response would be appropriate.

Abruptly breaking the spell, Simon extended one hand to the man standing on his left. As if by magic, the hand was filled with banknotes. With a flourish, Simon laid ten one hundred dollar bills on the glass.

A strangled exclamation escaped Larken and she swept through the curtain into the back. Sylvie, perched on a stool by the cash register, watched Simon with pointed curiosity.

"That's too much," River protested, pushing part of the money back to him.

"Nonsense. It is worth that and more to my mother. I insist."

Sylvie hastened to wrap the necklace as River numbly placed the money into the cash register and quickly wrote out a bill of sale.

"Now, enough business. On to pleasure. Have dinner with me this evening. It will be wonderful."

"Oh, I don't think so," River demurred. "I'm just settling in..."

"Please, don't make me beg," he chided. "A simple dinner is all I ask. I'm a hardworking man; surely you would not deny me this small pleasure. Plus, we need to talk some business, about the future of the store now that Deidre has been taken from us."

River mulled it over as she remembered how much she owed him. He had encouraged her rise from stringer to designer at a Virginia store, then later suggested her as manager for this store. He was also one of her best customers, having bought many of her designs during the past few years. And he could prove a useful contact when it came time to open her own business.

"All right," she agreed finally. "I would like that, only you mustn't keep me out too late, I'm afraid I overdid the sightseeing last night."

"Agreed!" he said, dark eyes snapping with excitement. "I will pick you up this evening—at eight."

He bussed her cheek in farewell and moved toward the door, the wrapped necklace held discreetly by one of his men.

"Wait! You'll need my address," River called.

Simon smiled. "This is my town, sweet River. I know where you live." With a nod of his sleek head, he was gone.

River and Sylvie stared at one another, shocked victims of a Minorca hurricane.

"Well," River muttered with a sigh, bending to rearrange the case emptied by Simon.

CHAPTER TWENTY

As usual, Johosh sneaked up on Larken while she was busy doing something else, in this case, sweeping the garage.

"Jesus, Jo! Will you learn to drive up to the house like everyone else? Where's your truck?" She cupped both hands over the broomstick and tried to slow her pounding heart.

Jo smiled. "Just keeping you on your toes. I parked around the corner."

Larken stowed the broom away and closed the garage door. "I'm really glad you agreed to this. I'm just real nervous about going through Dee's private stuff, you know?"

Jo nodded. "It is kind of a gray legal area. How you got it and all."

"Well, if you think I was gonna leave it for Minorca's goons, you got another thing coming," she said as she led the way around to the back of the estate and to the steps leading up to her apartment. "You know as well as I do that she wouldn't want them in her papers."

"I agree but what about her parents...and Evan?" Johosh shut the door firmly behind them.

"I plan to turn it all over," Larken said peevishly. "I just have to prepare myself...I gotta see how much of my livelihood Minorca owns."

"So, where is it?" Johosh asked, taking a seat at the table.

Larken went to the coat closet just off the living room and brought out the lockbox and computer. "Here's everything I saw. I haven't even touched it yet because I wanted to wait until you were here."

"What do you expect to find?" Johosh asked as he pulled the papers from the center of the laptop and looked them over.

Larken shrugged as she fiddled with the latch on the lockbox. "I don't know. Maybe the contract she signed with Minorca."

Johosh paused and studied Larken. "Minorca's legal team will have a copy of it. You know that, right?"

Larken sighed and pushed the lockbox away in disgust. "Duh! Look are you just here to give me grief? If that's the case, just go on back to Plantation. I'll do this by myself."

Jo studied her for a long beat. "So, someone is in a bad mood."

"What's your opinion on love, Jo?" Larken asked abruptly, seating herself and spinning the lockbox in her hands. "I mean, being a bachelor and all, you must have some pretty strong feelings about women in general," she finished, eyes twinkling with mischief.

Johosh eyed Larken with cool thoughtfulness before answering. "I don't know. They've always been a puzzlement to me. I guess if truth be told, women scare the bejeezus out of me." He laughed and picked self-consciously at a thumbnail. "No offense."

"Yeah, some of them scare me too. Especially those real pretty ones who know just how far their looks will take them."

"What's brought all this about?" Johosh asked quietly, glancing sideways at his friend.

"Never mind. Let's just get this thing open. Any ideas?"

"Use a nail and push the pins out the back side, the hinges."

Larken looked at Johosh doubtfully then studied the box. "No shit?"

"No shit," Jo replied calmly.

Larken made a face as she fetched her toolbox from the bottom of the same coat closet. Within minutes the lockbox was open and Johosh and Larken peered in.

"Damn," muttered Johosh.

"Damn is right." Larken lifted out five hefty stacks of money then a black velvet jeweler's pouch. She opened it and out spilled a yellowed strand of pearls, still on the original silk cord, a large diamond clustered dinner ring and two sets of earrings; one a child's first diamond chips and the other a large set of teardrop diamonds set in gold. Another shake released a tiny child's bangle of etched gold.

Jo whistled in appreciation as he touched one of the teardrops. "Do you think those are the originals or paste copies?"

"I think they're originals," Larken answered quietly. "Dee hated banks. Remember how she paid you by money order that time you helped her find that deadbeat?"

Jo nodded. "What's that there?" he asked.

"I have no idea," Larken said, reaching to pull the only remaining item, an envelope, from the bottom of the box. She turned it over and to her surprise, she found her name written across it in Dee's flowery handwriting.

"Whoa!" Jo muttered. "Let's see."

Nervously, her hands suddenly shaking, Larken opened the envelope.

CHAPTER TWENTY-ONE

It was almost eight o'clock and River had yet to decide what to wear to dinner. She had showered, dried her hair and applied light cosmetics, but the right dress kept eluding her. Every time she tried to visualize herself in a garment, Larken's scowling face filled her mind.

She had been horrible that afternoon after Simon left the store. Every word clipped and curt, bead bins slammed with random abuse, and she seemed to be avoiding everyone. Lunch had been a tense affair and both Sylvie and River had been overjoyed to see her leave early.

What had she done now to make Larken angry? How was she supposed to work with someone she couldn't even understand? Though she tried to lay the fault at Simon's door, she still felt as though Larken was angry with her for some imagined slight.

But only that morning they had seemed so...so comfortable together.

Looking down, River was dismayed to see she had pulled most of her clothing from the closet and flung the dresses, blouses and jackets into a haphazard pile on the floor.

"Damn! Damn!" she muttered, feeling a new sense of frustration fill her. Why did things, especially Larken, have to be so difficult? Why couldn't they be close? Be friends? River certainly could use a friend in this new environment.

Impulsively she lifted a spandex sheath of deep forest green from the pile and pulled it over her head. The dress, a gift from her last boyfriend, reminded her again of man's fickle nature. How appropriate, she thought, for no doubt Simon was typical of his kind.

Suddenly she didn't feel like going to dinner with him. She didn't feel like going anywhere, except maybe to bed with a good book.

A loud knock at the door sent her into a panic. Realizing she was still barefoot, she slipped into a pair of low-heeled black pumps and jerked a black lace shawl from a hook inside the closet door.

When she opened the door, she was surprised to see one of the men who normally accompanied Simon.

"Where's Mr. Minorca?" she asked, leaning to peer into the dim hall behind the large man.

"He sent me to pick you up, miss. I hope you don't mind." The man's voice was pleasant and even, very solicitous.

"And who are you?" She eyed him carefully.

"My name is Tim, ma'am, and I've worked for Mr. Minorca for seven years now. He trusts me completely and I hope you will too."

"Well, Tim, where will you be taking me?"

"To the Minorca estate, Miss Tyler. Mr. Minorca has had a meal prepared for you there. He planned to come himself but was detained by an overseas phone call. He sends his apologies."

River studied Tim's earnest, pleasant face. "Okay, Tim, let me get my bag."

Making sure she had her keys and her wallet in a small velvet bag, River switched off the light, closed the door, and allowed Tim to escort her to the waiting limousine.

CHAPTER TWENTY-TWO

The Minorca estate was located on the island's eastern shore, the long, palm-studded asphalt drive passing for half a mile along the shoreline. The house itself was crafted in typical Florida villa style, outer clapboards painted a pastel peach with plenty of white trim around the windows, doors, and wide front porch. Parked to one side were several expensive cars, half hidden by an abundance of tropical greenery. Pampas grass, a particular favorite of River's, did much to liven what would have been a dead sandscape of front yard.

As she stepped from the limousine into the gloom of evening, River was glad to see several cozy lights flicker to life in some of the house windows.

Then Simon was there, standing in the doorway, an Asian butler at his side.

"And you're here at last, my pet! Please accept my apologies for not coming for you myself. I had this business... Well, no matter. You look ravishing, positively decadent."

He drew the shawl from her shoulders, the bag from her hand and handed both to the butler who disappeared into the back.

Leaning forward, Simon pressed his lips to her cheek in a lingering caress. His warm breath disturbed tendrils of hair near her ear causing gooseflesh to rise across her skin.

"I'm so glad you came to me, my beautiful River," he breathed into her ear.

Tucking her arm beneath his, the silk of his shirt sliding deliciously across her bare flesh, Simon led her through the foyer. "Come now, I will show you my home. A home that I wish you would consider yours."

He paused and turned to face her, his face very close to hers. "I do not say that lightly, my dear. I hope you understand that."

"Oh, but..." River began, only to be interrupted as Simon continued.

"Ah, we won't talk of such things now. This is my office. I prefer to work from my home as much as possible. A good base as I travel so much. It's amazing how modern technology has made the world a much smaller place. What with facsimile machines, computers and modems, I feel no need to leave my home unless it's by choice. I have all the amenities here. Though the front of this place seems poor, I can assure you everything you could possibly want can be found right here within this home; my castle, if you will."

River tuned out the sound of Simon's interminable chatter and studied the office as they strolled through. He did seem to possess the latest in high-tech office equipment, all settled tastefully into a vaguely masculine decor. Books lined one wall but by their crisp spines and carefully planned layout, she could tell they were not well loved. A television-centered entertainment center dominated a second wall and a third wall bore a large ornate desk and the fourth a wealth of leather furniture situated into a conversation area.

"It's very nice," she murmured when a break in words presented itself.

"Why, thank you, my dear," he said, beaming proudly.

The two meandered through the villa and Simon swung open doors into a huge family room, several guest baths, a large fully-equipped kitchen currently occupied by a formal white-clad staff, and a very large dining room with a massive table, at least sixteen feet in length. The table was elaborately appointed with crystal stemware, sparkling plates and gleaming silver. Huge white camellia blooms floated in a clear bowl of water in the center of the table and their scent seemed to drug her with overpowering sweetness.

The tour finished here and Simon gallantly held her chair then took his place to her left.

"Ahh, this is nice. I enjoy having you here with me. After dinner, we shall explore the gardens in back and perhaps even the bedroom wing. Eh?"

He leered at her then laughed as if at some private joke. River, made nervous by his remark, glanced about the dining room. "And your mother? I thought she would be joining us."

Simon sighed and sipped from his water glass. "Alas, she feels poorly and has called in her personal masseuse to work out a few aches and pains." His frowned briefly then brightened. "You shall meet her though, very soon. She is a wonderful woman. I'm sure the two of you will hit it off excellently."

Leaning to one side, he depressed a button on the wall. A tinkling chime sounded, followed by soft, melodic music.

"Now, my River, tell me, how has your family taken to your leaving home?"

River chatted amiably while Simon's staff moved in and out setting up an incredible meal for the two of them.

"So I guess one less mouth to fill around home will be better for everyone," she finished, eyes widening at the amount of food arranged before her.

Simon nodded. "Yes, I suppose one must leave the nest sooner or later. Go on, my dear, eat, eat."

River eyed the low bowl directly before her uncertainly. "Umm, Simon, what is this?"

"Ahh, this? This is one of the island's specialties, lobster bisque. It's a type of lobster stew with a cream base. Very delicious, give it a try."

River dubiously lifted her soup spoon. To be polite, she lifted a token few bites but the heavy taste soon put her off. A salad, more to her liking, sat to her right, so with a pointed smile of appreciation to Simon, she moved the soup aside and began consuming the salad in earnest.

"Wait, my love, you must try the pepper parmesan dressing. It is fabulous. I had it made especially for you."

River, who enjoyed a good salad plain, reluctantly drew the bowl of creamy dressing closer. She poured a tiny bit on the vegetables and discovered it to be tasty, especially when used sparingly to complement the greens.

Next was a large tender-looking slab of beef, still leaking warm vital fluids onto the plate. She managed to ignore it and focus on the steamed vegetables and asparagus tips placed around the bloody centerpiece. Hot, crusty rolls rounded out River's meal.

"What?" Simon cried suddenly, peering at her plate. "The beef is not cooked to your liking? Why didn't you say so? I can have another sent out."

"Oh, no, please," River protested. "I just don't care for meat, is all. My family is vegetarian and raised me that way."

"How offended you must be by my thoughtlessness," Simon exclaimed as he reached to press the button again.

A server appeared immediately.

"Please take this plate away. Miss Tyler doesn't care for meat. Please remember this in the future," he told the waiter in a cool, low voice.

"Would you care for something else?" he asked River. "There is fish and chicken. Or perhaps you would care for fruit?"

River laughed nervously, overwhelmed by his solicitousness. "No, please, I'm satisfied. I think perhaps I'll just have another of these delicious rolls."

She smiled at the waiter, trying to reassure him, as she leaned to lift another fragrant hunk of bread from the basket next to her plate.

The waiter, endeared by her manner, smiled as if they shared a secret and moved quietly from the room.

"Are you sure, River?" he asked, laying his hot palm across the back of her hand. "Please tell me if you desire anything, anything at all. I am here to please you; I want you to understand that."

River's heart lurched into her throat as he moved his fingers sensuously along her hand and forearm. A subtle message was conveyed and River wondered suddenly what it would be like to give herself to this sleek, well-appointed man. He even smelled delicious, his cologne light and obviously expensive.

Should she ally with this man? She would never have to worry about money again, for Simon was one of the wealthiest men on the East Coast. It would certainly help her achieve her dream of opening her own store. For a brief moment she let the fantasy have free rein as his hand moved with sensual promise along her arm.

Then she remembered the ruthless means he was rumored to use to gain and keep his money and the dream abruptly burst. She gently extricated her hand and placed it safely in her lap.

"Simon," she said shakily, "we are business associates. Surely it would be unwise to make more of it than that."

Simon drew back, cupped his chin in his hand and watched her with dark, thoughtful eyes. "Perhaps I move too fast. I am too forward. There is one thing I wish you to know, however."

He leaned toward her so his face was very close. "I want you for my wife, River. That is why I have brought you here to my island."

River was further disconcerted. "But me, your wife? Why?"

He laughed and sat back again. "It's simple. Look in the mirror, my love. You are an incredibly beautiful woman, perfect for me. You will be an asset to my business and I can assure you, you will never want for anything. Ever. I promise you this. Agree to be my wife and I will shower you with your heart's desire. Bear my sons and you will win a permanent place in my heart. Be my lover and I will give you ecstasy beyond compare." He watched her with smoldering eyes, causing River's skin to flame as she colored from head to toe.

"Oh, I have embarrassed you. Your innocence is so charming, another of your many attributes. There, I will talk no more of such things. Think on what I have said and you will come to me when you are ready."

Simon returned to his food, eating with gusto now that he had made his intentions clear. River took a long, choking drink of her iced tea, her mind racing.

CHAPTER TWENTY-THREE

After coffee and a dessert of silky key lime pie, Simon and River walked through the extensive gardens behind the house.

The back of the estate was quite different from the front, filled with lush greenery in beds of imported topsoil. A long vegetable garden stretched the length of one side and wisteria, bougainvillea and passionflower vines climbed the side of the house, in the evening's dimness. Beds of creamy gardenias sweetened the air. Fruit trees shimmered in the ocean wind and flowers danced in every available space.

Struck by the well-landscaped beauty lit by floodlights and lanterns along the pathways, forgetting for a brief moment the decision she must make, River rushed forward to brush flower blooms with her fingers. "This is so wonderful! Do you do this yourself?"

Simon watched her delight with shuttered eyes, arms folded across his chest like a sultan surveying his empire.

"Unfortunately, business concerns keep me from active gardening. The design is mine however, and I do come here often to unwind. So you like it?"

River smiled and examined a lime tree, the leaves leaving a delicious citrus scent on her hands. "Of course. It's incredible."

"Good. It shall be yours. Come with me now, I want to show you the pool."

River followed obediently until she realized they were entering what he had referred to earlier as the bedroom wing. But she entered into a huge glass-walled enclosure with a pool, hot tub and gym.

"This is where I like to come and take care of my body. We only have one temple you know, so we must care for it properly."

River strolled forward to look into the pool. The water which she had expected to be clear blue, was instead a dusky blue and murky.

"Sea water," Simon said just behind her. "It's filtered but I do find the salt refreshing, the minerals replenishing. Won't you go for a swim with me? There is an assortment of suits in the dressing room."

River shook her head. "No, really, I mustn't. I still haven't recovered completely from my move I'm afraid," she added apologetically.

"Forgive me. I chatter on and here you are yawning. Let's get you home now and we will swim another time, when the sun can bathe our shoulders with heat."

Within minutes, they were in the backseat of Simon's limousine, prowling like a black shark through the brightly lit streets of downtown Key West. Simon walked River to her door and gave her a lingering kiss on the cheek.

"Thank you for dining with me, River. I hope you have had a good time."

River opened her door and turned to face him. "Yes, the food was delicious and you have a lovely home. Thank you for an enjoyable evening."

He kissed his fingertips and waved them toward her. "Until next time then. Sleep well."

River pressed the door shut. Dropping her bag on the floor, she leaned her back against the door, expelling all the breath in her lungs. Simon wanted her for a wife! *Sheesh!* Things were getting weirder and weirder. And they hadn't even discussed the future of Designs by Deidre at all.

Larken, dripping sweat, hair plastered to her cheeks, watched Simon's glossy limousine pull away from the curb in front of River's apartment building. Well, he hadn't stayed, thank goodness. Still, she was angry with both of them, flaunting their affair right there in front of everyone in the shop.

She rocked the bicycle she'd been riding back and forth between her muscular thighs, staring thoughtfully at River's kitchen window. Larken wanted to see her, to tell her goodbye. She had a fixed desire to see River's rosy lips curl in a smile and to see her icy eyes melt with pleasure.

The kitchen light flickered into life and she spied River as she walked across to the refrigerator. She was wearing the same shortened T-shirt she'd worn that night on Mallory Pier, her lean midriff gleaming in the kitchen light.

Larken fancied she could see the bikini panties River wore, imagining them made from white lace, riding high up on the sides of her long legs, and a sudden ache for her began to grow deep in the center of Larken's body.

Deeply disturbed, she pulled her gaze from the window and pedaled her bike with rapid haste away along Petronia Street.

CHAPTER TWENTY-FOUR

The next few days passed at a snail's pace. Business at Designs by Deidre was slow as the south Florida summer approached and snowbirds began returning to their homes in the north.

As her life settled into a routine, River fretted about whether or not to marry Simon. She rose early each morning, jogged through the awakening downtown streets, then worked long hours at the store. Evenings were spent either at Mallory Pier sitting beside Beebee, or at home alone curled up with a book borrowed from the tiny town library.

Conspicuously absent from her life was Larken Moore.

She'd been the one to find the cryptic note Monday morning. Larken had left it on the worktable in back. *Gone to Arizona for beads*, it said, *be back in a week or so*. Larken's name was printed at the bottom in bold black letters.

Alone in the store, River had indulged herself by running a fingertip over the forceful letters etched hard into the piece of paper.

Larken.

Why was she so drawn to her? Goodness knows she hadn't encouraged River's friendship in any way. There was something about her though, a special quality of stoic tenderness, a quality highly evident the night she'd cared for her after the musician's attack. Without obsequious displays of solace, Larken had soothed her in a way that had helped her heal emotionally as well as spiritually.

Now Larken was three days gone and River found herself missing deeply that quiet, calm presence.

Then there was the troubling dilemma concerning Simon Minorca. She had his unusual marriage proposal to consider. He sent her a flower—a rose—as a reminder each day. She knew he was impatiently awaiting her answer and that knowledge hung like an unsteady ax over her head.

She should tell him no outright, she told herself several times a day. Then the nagging little voice of selfishness would intrude. This might be the only chance, the little voice would warn, to have no money worries ever again, to afford the store you've been dreaming about for so many years. A road filled with hard work faced her if she turned down Simon's proposal. She would have to work her way up slowly, not always an easy task. Moreover, to her shame, her eyes were misted by the ease a life with Simon would bring.

But her eyes weren't misted enough to overlook Minorca's way of life. She didn't know specifics for sure, but if what the gossips back in Virginia said could be believed, Simon was part of a mafia-type organization that specialized in all types of illegal business, including gambling, drugs and prostitution. Was this something she wanted to bring into her life?

Sighing, River peeked through the curtained doorway and saw that Sylvie was still minding the empty store. The young girl was perched atop a tall stool next to the cash register, totally engrossed in a paperback mystery.

At least the lack of business was giving River time to foster her creative impulses. For days now she had been studying the island sunsets, wondering how best to manifest the scenes into a piece of jewelry.

The major holdup to the piece's inception was finding the right shade of red as a guiding base. Absently, since she had this free time, she began prowling the long tables searching for just the right hue. She rejected coral as too orange, garnet as too purple, red jasper as too brown. Half an hour later nothing had presented itself and she began to despair.

She strode to the back of the room to the large jeweler's vault that dominated the storeroom. Using the key carried on a coiled bracelet around her wrist, she disengaged the lock of the heavy door and pushed it open. Eyes wandering across the many rows of black boxes, River instinctively chose one and pulled it down but found it contained clear crystals, something she didn't need. Another held small diamond chips and a third, amber. Finally, three boxes later, she found the perfect stones.

Gazing down into the black velvet case filled with swirled, iridescent opals, River caught her breath and spent a full minute studying their beauty, imagining how she would form the necklace. She reverently set that box aside and continued her search.

An hour later she sat engrossed in her work. She took each of the chosen opal cabochons, some twenty in number, and with glue and patience set each one into an embossed gold foil setting that had delicate little ears so it could be strung together with other beads. While these dried, she laid out several ten-millimeter cinnabar beads from China. Cinnabar was an ore base of mercury that bore a deep, rich red color. These she spaced out on her bead board. At the bottom of the necklace she added several dark spacer beads of red carnelian in between the cinnabar. An opal, the brittle, delicate stone full of the rich swirled color of the sky at sunset, would be inserted between each cinnabar bead and highlighted on each side by six-millimeter brown goldstone beads—russet colored and full of bright copper flecks. Four lemon yellow Czechoslovakian glass beads spaced evenly would finish it. Perfect.

The piece planned, she lost herself in the construction, not even hearing Sylvie say she had closed the shop and was going home. River's head never lifted until ten o'clock that evening when every last eye pin had been fastened to every last bead. What she ended up with was a loose concoction, much like a rosary, but, by color and style, with serious Art Deco leanings. The looseness ensured that each slight movement caught light and dazzled the eye. It was beautiful, her loveliest piece to date.

Sudden spasms stabbed furiously between her shoulder blades as she wearily filed away her tools, findings, and unused beads. Reaching up onto a high shelf, she located the Polaroid camera and snapped a photo of the necklace for the reference book of originals kept by the store, and then stashed the necklace onto a shelf of the vault. She would give it to Len or Sylvie in the morning and they would draw a blueprint of Mallory, as she had named the necklace, so it could be re-created.

She frowned at the necklace as she placed it into the vault. This was an expensive one. The opals, collected from mines in Australia were costly, as was the imported cinnabar. Nevertheless, she knew that it had to be this way, no matter the cost. Anything less would be a lie. Yawning, River snapped off the light and let herself out, making sure she locked the doors securely, and began the walk home through still busy Key West streets.

CHAPTER TWENTY-FIVE

A loud knock sounding on her apartment door woke her several hours later. Looking at the clock, she saw it was past two a.m. Panic coursed through her.

Leaping up she realized she was still naked, having fallen into bed directly after her shower, so she shrugged into her robe even as she scrubbed sleep from her eyes.

"Who is it?" she cried at the door as the insistent knock was repeated.

"Larken. Let me in now!"

Larken? What was she doing back in town so early? Hastily she pushed the questions aside and unlocked the door. Larken sounded angry. And she *was* angry. River could tell by Larken's finger-tousled hair and snapping green eyes.

"Please, come in," River told her, stepping back and

gesturing her in as any hostess would do, even though it was an unreasonable hour.

Larken stepped into the dimness of River's apartment and began pacing in the small living room. She was wearing shorts and tank top under an opened button-down shirt that slapped like wings with each pass she made. Her hair was wet and the shorts bore damp patches.

"I came home early because...well, because...and I go to my house. Then because I can't sleep, I decide to carry my satchel over to the store to unload it. What do I find?"

She swung hooded, predatory eyes around and impaled River with them.

River stood numb, mind racing as she tried to figure out what calamity she had caused. The doors had been locked, she was sure of it.

"I have no idea, Larken, you'll have to tell me," she said finally, crossing her arms in resignation.

"Someone," she turned and paced in the other direction, "and I think I know just the someone, has used almost all my precious opals. Do you know how hard these opals are to acquire, lady? Do you know how I have to bust my hump just to get a few of these beauties? Hot days in the Outback, in a smelly hovel, bargaining with crooks. Do you know what that's like?"

River watched Larken with open-mouthed amazement. "No, Larken," she said with unnatural calm, swallowing the first surges of outrage. "Why don't you tell me what it's like."

"It's..." she began, pausing when River's calmness penetrated her ire. "It's bad, okay?"

River walked toward the kitchen and fetched herself a glass of water from the refrigerator. "Seems to me, Larken," she said in a flat, steely voice, "you're in the wrong line of business if you dislike the job so much."

Now it was Larken's turn to stand with mouth agape. "Does that mean what I think it means? Are you threatening me?"

River eyed her with confusion. "With what? Threatening you with what?"

"Threatening my job," she thundered. "You can't fire me,

you know. No one can do that." Larken glared at her, a challenge bright in her snapping eyes.

"Larken." River was tired and not in the mood for any more doubletalk. "I don't know what you are talking about. The thought of firing you never even entered my head. Why don't you just go home and get some sleep. We can talk about this tomorrow when we're both a bit calmer and more well-rested."

"Oh, don't pull that Miss Sensible crap on me. I want to know who gave you the right to go into that vault and just use whatever the hell you pleased? Suppose some of those beads were reserved for someone?"

Alarm jangled along River's nerves. She hadn't thought of that possibility. She lifted her chin high in defiance.

"I can't help that, Larken, but in the future, we'll have to make sure reserved beads are well marked so this won't happen again. Who were the beads being held for?"

In her imagination she saw dollar signs take wing as she wondered how she would purchase replacements if Mallory didn't sell right away.

Larken didn't answer, but moved to stand gazing out the front window at the dim street outside. She seemed deeply troubled.

"Larken?"

She turned and gazed evenly at River. "No one. But suppose they had been, River, what would we have done then?"

"Whatever we had to do. Why must you be such a pessimist? Didn't you see what I made with the opals?" Her voice rose with excitement as she studied Larken's frowning face.

A person shouldn't be allowed to look this good at two in the morning, a part of her whispered, especially when they're angry. She noted the satiny dark hair feathering on Larken's shoulders, eyes following down and fastening on small, pointed breasts battling the thin undershirt. Blushing, she lifted her gaze, noticing how well shaped the dark slashing eyebrows were and how finely her nose cleaved the dimness of the room.

"Stop looking at me!" Larken muttered suddenly, turning from the window. "Don't look at me with those eyes."

Those eyes? What the hell did she mean by that?

River whirled and walked toward the kitchen. "Well," she said, her back to the other woman, "did you or did you not see the necklace?"

"You mean this?" Larken drew the necklace from the front pocket of her shirt and held it aloft, light from the street gathering energy and shooting away from the beads.

River looked back and gave a small shriek of alarm. "Oh, Larken, please, I spent hours on that, please don't break it."

Larken looked at River as if she'd gone mad. Then she reconsidered and devilment leapt in her face. "It would serve you right if I did, you know."

She placed both hands within the circle of beads. "I could snap out and beads would go flying, wouldn't they?"

River swallowed and licked her lips nervously. Part of her wanted to challenge Larken's bluff but the woman was still an unknown entity to her. How could she be sure Larken wouldn't really destroy it? Tears of indecision welled in her eyes. One escaped the pool and cascaded frantically along her cheek. With an impatient gesture she brushed the moisture away and watched Larken defiantly.

Larken weakened as the tear sparkled in the light shining between the open drapes. "Oh, hey, I'm...I'm sorry, River. I wouldn't break it. Really. It's too beautiful." Her voice lowered to a whisper. "Almost as beautiful as you."

The words that until this moment River hadn't realized she'd been longing to hear, staggered her. A thrill surged through her body. Surprise at the sudden feeling must have mirrored itself on her face for Larken moved toward her. They were in each other's arms then, River wondering how it happened, and Larken was dragging the doubled strand of opals and cinnabar along River's neck. The feel of the smooth cool beads sent a chill along River's spine, raising gooseflesh and tickling deliciously.

Larken splayed her hands, one still holding the necklace, on either side of River's head and pulled her close. Her hot mouth captured River's lips and the kiss was deep, causing River's knees to collapse until Larken had to support her weight. The kiss lasted a wondrous epoch until Larken finally broke away, her breathing ragged and her whispered voice hoarse.

"Send me away, River. Tell me to go home. I can't do it by myself. You have to send me away."

River, standing where the other had left her, lifted one hand and fingered her lips. She felt as if she were trying to move through a heated pool, her limbs heavy and the cleft between her legs bearing a strange ache she'd never felt before. She lifted eyes filled with wonder and darkened by passion.

"I can't," she whispered with a small shrug of her shoulders and an apologetic smile. "I can't."

Larken approached her slowly, dark eyes burning. Lifting the necklace over River's glowing hair, she draped its heaviness around her neck then stood back to admire it.

"Yes," she whispered musingly, "you go together. When I saw it I knew I had to see it on you."

Moving still closer, she pulled at the belt of River's robe until it came loose. Gently she slid it from her shoulders, letting the soft fabric pool at their feet. Her indrawn breath was sharp but she watched with frank appreciation until River's shyness passed and, delighting in her woman's shape, she held herself proudly. Larken moaned deep in her throat and reached reverently to cup one small, well-rounded breast. River's head fell back as the warmth of the hand swept through her.

"Oh, Larken," she breathed.

Larken sighed in response and both hands reached to caress sides and waist, running slowly down until circling to grasp the smooth buttocks. With gentle roughness she pulled River close.

River gasped as their lean bodies fit together; soft breasts, hot bellies, legs meshing, sensations she'd never felt before.

Holding River close, Larken let her fingers comb thick hair and rub the soft pulse of River's neck. The stiffened tips of River's breasts teased with tantalizing torture. She inhaled River's clean, citrus scent and knew that this first time would be intense. She tried to calm herself. If River had never made love to a woman before, Larken wanted this first time to be incredible for her.

Pressing her cheek to the softness of River's, she had to know. "Have you ever...?"

River smiled as she reached and unfastened the shorts separating them, her hands lingering as they slid the fabric along Larken's slim hips. "Not yet."

Larken's body, released by River's touch and her words, pulsed with new intensity.

River's body was afire and she knew she had to be naked with this woman right now, this instant. Never in her life had she been so aroused by a simple touch, so excited by another's proximity.

She swept clothing away so her hands could graze across the delicious expanse of breast and skin. Larken was so well-muscled, each length of cord defined and firmly smooth beneath the soft, soft skin. River ached to get inside. She gave her mouth free rein and she suckled one small, erect nipple, her tongue lolling across tight skin as she sought the other one.

Larken moaned and pushed her away. "Ahh, no," she whispered, "you vixen."

River giggled softly and pushed hard at Larken's waist until she fell back onto the sofa. Her look of surprise delighted River as she spread her legs and straddled the pliant, sensually alive body. Both gasped as skin connected and River stilled to enjoy the new sensations.

Her lips sought the soft mouth again as Larken's hands played across her body, flowing, brushing sensitive peaks. The kiss lengthened; lasted hours, years. Both women seemed to forget time as their bodies warmed together.

River began to move. She had never loved a woman but her body recalled a distant, primal memory and moved with abandon. Larken obligingly moved her own body upward, as if delighting in the pressure of her lover's warm wetness against her thigh, as if gaining intense satisfaction from River's pleasure.

Larken turned her face away and lay her head along the back of the sofa, her jaw clenched tightly. River paused doubtfully and lifted Larken's hand, bringing it back to her breast. Larken's eyes opened and River felt deeply touched by the tenderness glowing there.

She leaned forward and softly kissed Larken again, giving back that emotion threefold. A silent but powerful communication passed between them and a smile lifted the corners of Larken's lips.

Larken surprised River by leaning forward and latching her mouth onto first one breast peak, then the other, suckling deeply, her strong fingers cupping and indenting the soft flesh on each side. The sudden sensation sent River over the edge. Spasms emerged from somewhere deep and it was as though the feeling was going to wrench her apart. Cries escaped her lips and she knew that if Larken left her at that moment she would die, simply die and the explosion within would never happen.

Larken allowed River to fall onto the softness of the sofa next to her. Arching her own body, Larken, still loving River's breasts, slid one hand down along her lover's flat belly. The hand crept lower still and made a home for itself in the soft, sea-foam folds of River's sex.

A startled moan sounded from River as Larken's touch carried her closer and closer to a precipice. Then Larken forgot everything except the drive that kept her moving, pulling out River's pleasure until she rocked with completion.

Larken's lips sought River's as River collapsed under her. They breathed into each other, waiting for sanity to return.

CHAPTER TWENTY-SIX

The call of peacocks and cooing of peahens in the lawn outside brought Larken into full awareness. It was barely dawn. They were cuddled together on River's bed. River's platinum hair lay fanned out across Larken's chest and the scent of it was comforting to her. She realized how much she had come to feel about River in the short time they'd known one another. Last night had been the culmination of the growing feelings between them. It frightened Larken, while making her heart soar at the same time. Sudden thoughts of Minorca intruded, causing her chest to constrict. Would he take River from her? How deep was their involvement?

River stirred and lifted her head to gaze sleepily at Larken.

"Hi. What time is it?"

"Good morning. Early. Not yet light."

River tucked her head. "God, you must think I'm horrible after last night."

Larken chuckled and kissed River's hair. "No, baby. I think you're wonderful. Why would you think otherwise?"

"The way I acted. I've never...been like that before." She sat and pulled the sheet up to cover her nakedness.

"I'll take that as a compliment." She paused a long beat before continuing. "I'm glad you let me love you. I was so afraid but wanted you in my arms so badly."

"So, we're okay?" She peeked at Larken from the parted curtain of her hair.

"Oh, yeah. Very okay. But I have to tell you, being together last night really threw me too," she confessed. "I'd never reacted to anyone quite that way before."

River smiled in the dimness, one finger idly plucking at the tight flesh of Larken's arm. "Is that why you were so mean to me that first day? Because you were afraid of me? I thought it was because you plain didn't like me."

Larken smoothed her hair. "Yeah, I guess I was overcompensating for the attraction. I'm sorry I was so mean."

Dark thoughts invaded Larken's mind but she pushed them away, reluctant to spoil the bliss of their time together.

"I'll forgive you if you'll tell me you like my necklace," River cajoled, fingering the heavy necklace still draped around her neck.

Larken turned on her side so she was facing River. Her warm breath fanned across River's eyes. "I do like your necklace. I like all your necklaces and you know what?"

"What?"

"I like you. God help me, even though I know better."

River bristled. "Why? What do you mean?"

Larken's hand crept low on her stomach, stopping to cup the softly furred mound of River's womanhood in one strong hand. Gently she moved the hand until the other's breathing increased and the question was swept away.

"Now we'll take our time," she whispered against soft lips. "Touch me, River."

River touched her, opening the door to another dimension where passion reigned supreme.

CHAPTER TWENTY-SEVEN

The tall, thin woman moved like a lioness, with a strange, lanky prowl not normally associated with humans. River noticed her—indeed, was hypnotized by her—as soon as the woman crossed through the store's glass-fronted exterior. This, she said silently to herself, is exactly the type of woman I would like to wear my jewelry.

The woman was on the high side of fifty but her hair, worn pulled back in a classic French twist, still bore the blonde of a younger woman. Not as brilliant perhaps, but a more subdued color as befitted her age. Her cosmetics appeared to have been applied by a professional; without being obvious, they still did much to improve and highlight her honey brown eyes, high Roman cheekbones and thin lips. Her clothing was simple yet exquisite, a classic Chanel suit in a deep burgundy perfectly matched to her leather pumps and clutch handbag.

As the customer's delightful perfume wafted to her nostrils, River noticed with joy the necklace adorning the woman's neck. It was the piece she'd first designed upon arriving in Florida; the necklace about sea, sand and sky. The swirling blues and tans blended perfectly with the style and color of the woman's suit. Upon seeing the piece, River understood who this elegant woman had to be: Simon Minorca's mother.

"Mrs. Minorca," River said with enthusiasm as she stepped from behind the counter to greet the newcomer. "It's so nice to meet you at last."

Mrs. Minorca was momentarily surprised but covered her confusion with a soft chuckle. "Ah, the necklace must have given me away. How sharp you are! But please call me Patrice. I insist."

River smiled. "Yes, it was the necklace. They're like children, you know. A mother always knows her child's face."

They stood silently sizing up one another, River nervously fiddling with the hem of her shorts. The other woman's elegance made her own simple outfit seem shabby.

Remembering her duties, River resumed her post behind the counter. "So, what can I show you this morning?"

"Actually, I was hoping you could get away for a brief lunch. I'd really like to get to know you. My son is quite taken with you, you know."

River was embarrassed and nervously tucked her head.

Patrice chuckled. "How dear you are and so beautiful with those eyes! So, come to lunch. Can you get away?"

"Yes, I believe I can leave for a little while. Let me check with Sylvie and make sure she'll be here. Today is Carter's day off."

With an uncertain smile River moved into the back room, her mind filled with questions. What was Simon Minorca's mother's agenda?

CHAPTER TWENTY-EIGHT

Patrice, and the driver, Tim, escorted River via limousine to a stylish restaurant called Nemann's. They were shown to a small, linen-draped table positioned next to a large glass wall overlooking the Gulf of Mexico. As if trying to help River relax, the older woman took charge. She ordered salads for both of them then sat back, gold cigarette case in hand. Lighting a thin cigarette in a genteel manner, she regarded River through a veil of exhaled smoke.

"So, Simon tells me he hasn't heard from you since his proposal two weeks ago. Is there a problem we should talk about? I can assure you Simon is a wonderful man."

River choked on her water. Was this woman always so blunt?

"I beg your pardon?" she stammered finally.

Patrice leaned forward, solicitously. "Oh, I am sorry. Perhaps that came out all wrong. I must tell you though, our household is on pins and needles awaiting your answer. We wish to start redecorating. Simon wishes to devote a whole area of the Key West home to you. He's so concerned about your happiness. So, tell me. Have you given his proposal some thought?"

"Well, of course," River replied quickly. "Such a major decision deserves a great deal of thought."

"And?"

A momentary reprieve came with the delivery of their salads and River had time to think and organize her feelings. Larken's strong face filled her mind. The memory of their night together made her feel languid and heated. That she had even considered the idea of marrying Minorca, a man she didn't love, seemed so foolish now. There was no way Simon could give her the passion that Larken had given her last night. Larken was her lover and she realized that in addition to the intense physical attraction she felt for her, she was beginning to fall in love with her, with her very essence. She admired Larken; her strength, her gentle willfulness, even the way she smiled so serenely. Yes, love had definitely seemed a possibility just that morning as they shared a tender, lingering kiss of farewell, perfectly topping off their night of intimacy.

Patrice was watching her with a puzzled frown. "Well?"

River shook off her romantic reverie and faced Patrice squarely. "Well, Mrs... Patrice, I'm afraid I'm going to turn down your son's proposal. I can't marry him."

Patrice impatiently pushed her nibbled salad aside, her expression turning fretful. "But why? Don't you understand what my son is offering you?"

River nodded and took a morsel of her own salad. She chewed as she thought, then dabbed her lips with her napkin before answering. She was stalling, trying to figure out a way to tell this woman how she really felt without causing unnecessary friction or causing trouble for Designs by Deidre. She had to be as diplomatic as possible.

"I'm afraid there is someone else who I've come to love. I don't love your son, but it is certainly no reflection on him as a person. If this other person had not come into my life," she said, "your son would have been a wonderful husband, I'm sure."

"But Simon has done so much for you," Patrice insisted.

"Yes, yes, that's true," River interjected hurriedly. "And I shall be forever grateful. I consider Simon a dear friend but surely that's not reason enough for marriage, is it?"

"Of course it is," Patrice said impatiently. "Do you think I loved Simon's father? Of course not. Our marriage was arranged by our families. Yet we had a perfectly satisfying life together until his death."

River, with her parents' own relationship as a guide, couldn't imagine a loveless one, although she was aware they existed.

"I appreciate that," she said, adding simply, "I just don't think that's for me."

Patrice Minorca, seeing the younger woman's resolve, decided to let the matter drop for the present. Delicately attacking her salad, she asked about River's life. She already knew the answers to the questions, of course; River had been investigated, as had every other woman in whom Simon had shown an interest. This knowledge gave her the opportunity to think, all the while making the appropriate polite responses, and a plan began to form. Surely this chit of a girl would love Simon if she were only given the opportunity to know him.

Lunch ended on a pleasant note but on the way back to Designs by Deidre, Patrice calmly and politely reminded River that Simon's company held a substantial investment in the store River currently managed.

"I do hope you will reconsider your decision, River dear. Change is such a nasty inconvenience."

"I'm not sure I know what you mean," River replied, a satisfying alarm tightening her voice.

"Well, surely you understand that my son, in his pain over your rejection of his proposal, could not bear to see you during the course of a day's business. Such sightings would prove awkward at best."

River turned her face away so she was staring from the tinted windows of the car. "I see," she said with a sigh, then added, "I will certainly think over what you have said."

Patrice sat back, one hand smoothing the fabric of her skirt.

CHAPTER TWENTY-NINE

Larken was working at the front counter when River returned to the store. Her green eyes lit with delight upon seeing River, then clouded.

River sensed the perceptible cooling and realized she must have seen the dark limousine pulling away from the curb just outside.

"What's wrong, Larken? Are you okay?"

Larken watched her with doubtful eyes for a long beat before dropping her gaze. Her strong hands fumbled with the pages of the inventory book as she struggled to close it.

"Larken?" River, forgetting her own dilemma, moved toward the other woman seeking intimacy, needing comfort.

Larken moved away.

"I'm fine, River. Did you have a nice lunch?"

So that *was* it. Larken thought she was with Simon and was jealous. River smiled at the ridiculous notion.

Larken glanced up and, obviously misinterpreting River's smile, stalked out of the store, through the curtained doorway to the back room then slamming through the employee entrance.

River stood rooted where Larken left her, numb and confused. Was there no reasoning with this woman? Why wouldn't she talk with her about this? Frustration grew.

Maybe coming to Key West had been a big mistake. Perhaps she wasn't savvy and mature enough to deal with business and with life bigger than that found in Bryant, Virginia, after all. She certainly hadn't been too successful thus far.

Tears welled as she chastised herself. Here she was, mooning over a co-worker, a woman, for goodness sake, even sleeping with this woman, and about to lose her new position as manager, possibly even her job, because she wouldn't marry one of her bosses. Why did her personal life have to interfere in her business life? Everything would be all right if she'd just managed to keep the two separate.

Then she remembered that business at Designs by Deidre had not exactly been booming since her arrival, either. And she had created only two pieces since coming to the new store, much reduced from her usual production of several pieces a month. Perhaps she was a failure as a manager as well; the store was not nearly as organized as she had expected it to be by this time.

Sylvie returned from her own lunch and entered the front of the store through the curtained doorway from the back room. Seeing River, her smile faded and she rushed to her side.

"Oh my gosh, what's wrong? Are you okay, River? What's happened?"

River, blinded by tears, could only grimace and shake her head. What could she tell Sylvie? That she had realized she was a failure? A harsh bark of laughter escaped. Sylvie probably already knew.

Sylvie was becoming seriously alarmed. "River, honey, I think maybe you better sit down." She hovered like a nervous mother hen but River broke away with a muttered apology.

"I'll be back, Syl, I can't...work now. Mind the store, okay? Please?"

Sylvie nodded, her face a mask of confusion and helplessness, and River bolted out the front door.

At first she jogged at an easy pace along the sidewalks of downtown Key West, trying to chase the frantic self-pity from her mind. When she reached the rocky western edge of the island at a slow walk, she calmed and began to think sensibly again. Foaming salt water, slapping against the coral base of the island, served to soothe her thoughts. Warm, fragrant winds, blowing inward from the sea, shaped her emotions and gave them definition.

She realized she should probably leave the island and return to the safe, known haven of Virginia. But it seemed too much like admitting defeat. No matter that the move made the most sense for all concerned, it still smacked of giving up. She needed to decide just how important her job managing Designs by Deidre was to her and what she was willing to tolerate.

Looming large in her mind was her new relationship with Larken. Never had she anticipated such a thing happening to her. She had been introduced to the idea of lesbianism at an early age. A great-aunt on her father's side had never married, certainly an oddity among her peers. Instead, the aunt's life had revolved around a female "companion" whom she had lived with until her death. When queried about this relationship, River's mother had taken River aside and explained it in the simplest terms: sometimes women love women and men love men. And that's okay because love is love and whatever makes people happy and content is what works for them.

River, curiosity appeased, had filed the information away and never judged those whose lifestyle differed from what she considered her norm. Now Larken had entered her life and without knowing it, the deepest emotion she'd ever felt for a person was blossoming into being. Her past relationships with men now seemed pale when compared with the passion she and Larken shared.

Obviously working with Larken was going to be very difficult, if not impossible, whether or not their relationship lasted. Should she try and forget about what had transpired between them and see Larken in a business sense only? Could she do this?

She lowered herself to a sitting position on a pile of coarse coral reef and let the foamy waves wash across her white sneakers. The water lapped at her like the warm, damp tongue of a dog, and was just as comforting. The constant sound of the traffic behind her harmonized well with the noisy upheaval of the sea below her.

No, she could not do this. Not when being near Larken made her heart race, fueled by the memory of their lovemaking. Not when Larken's every smile and nod of approval was becoming so important. She realized then how devastated she had been by Larken's sudden departure today when she had desperately needed reassurance and reaffirmation that what they had shared was real and special. Why did Larken have to be so cruel and ruled by such unreasonable jealousy? Her mind whirled with contradictions. If only River could banish Larken from her mind and her life things would be so much easier.

She again entertained the notion of marrying Simon. To accept his proposal would certainly take care of some problems but she was smart enough to realize that often solving one batch of problems opened a whole new batch. Would lying in Simon's arms help her forget Larken? She didn't think so. At this point, she feared she would never be able to shake Larken's serene image from her mind or heart.

She sighed and squinted at the bright sun straight above her. Its heat penetrated her entire body, soothing her anguish to some small degree.

She wondered suddenly what her next meeting with Simon would be like. Certainly tense. He would surely fire her, she decided, to help save face, and this was something else she would have to deal with in the near future.

CHAPTER THIRTY

With no easy answers forthcoming, River walked back inland toward the downtown area. Letting her mind wander, she allowed her feet to follow and soon found herself in the main street of a charming residential area. She passed Front Street with its defunct seafood canneries visible off in the distance. The next street was Greene and the name's familiarity nagged at her. With mounting excitement, she remembered seeing Greene Street listed as Larken's mailing address. She lived somewhere on this very street. Try as she would, River could not remember the number and so walked slowly along the tree-shaded lane, trying to guess which house was Larken's. Would it look like her, tall, simple, strong? She immersed herself in the game, happy for something that turned her mind from the gnawing problems she would soon be forced to deal with.

Several people passed by on the quiet street but she either ignored them with lowered glance or nodded politely as she walked past houses jumbled without rhyme or reason one almost atop another. At the second block, the houses abruptly played out and she was left facing a few scrubby lots that were empty but for realty signs.

She retraced her steps. Midway through the largest block, she saw a pleasantly constructed house that occupied a slightly bigger plot of land than most of the others. The small, tidy grounds were exquisitely landscaped and something about the arrangement struck her as Oriental, with a certain simple grace that whispered Larken to her.

Gingerly, feeling like a thief, River ducked between the tall hedges that set the property off from the paved road. She crept forward, studying the shuttered house which was vaguely Italianate in architecture, but with more terraces than usual for the traditional Italianate form. Staring up at the weathered two-story wooden structure, she wondered if Larken slept in this house each night, if this was her place of refuge from the world.

A muted slapping noise drew her attention and she followed the sound, stepping carefully around several low-limbed palm trees to the side of the house.

She saw Larken and a gasp of surprise almost gave her away.

The backyard of the house stretched to the sea on the farthest side. Carefully nurtured palms and clumps of the ever present pampas grass dotted the wide expanse of sandy land. Someone, probably Larken, had turned this haphazardly shaped area into a pleasant open-air gym. River spied a long line of nylon-covered dumbbells in all shapes and sizes. There was a thick balance beam and several long punching bags hung from poles covered with complicated rigging. A strange wooden, man-shaped contraption occupied one corner of the yard and wide boards wrapped with what looked like rope jutted vertically from the sandy soil at irregular intervals.

The slapping noise sounded again and River saw Larken lift her leg in a high sideways kick and slap the top of her right foot, with incredible power, against the side of one of the bags. A guttural cry escaped her at the moment of impact and that cry sent fear coursing through River.

Larken was comfortably dressed, wearing only a pair of loose fitting white trousers which came to just below her knee and a loose white T-shirt that left bare her lean midriff.

She was still angry; River could tell by the rapidity and force of her blows as she repeatedly attacked the bag. She feasted her eyes as the powerful woman moved through a rigorous workout. Her kicks were high and precisely placed and her blows seemed deadly.

After some time she stopped hitting the various bags and boards and stood dead still for a long time, fists clenched and arms held out before her. Just as River thought about creeping away, Larken began to move. At first through various exercises to ward off imaginary opponents. She fought thin air, her hands, wrists, elbows, knees and feet all coming into play as weapons. It was like ballet when she moved and River found herself entranced by her fluidity of form. But even this did not prepare her when Larken switched from violence into peace and moved through the most beautiful *T'ai Chi Chuan* form River had ever seen.

T'ai Chi, a form of Chinese meditation through motion, was something River herself practiced occasionally. Her parents and several of their friends practiced it, had taught it to her, but, though she had watched many move through the form, never had she seen it performed with such strength or economy of motion. Obviously Larken had been practicing for quite some time and had mastered all the intricate nuances of motion inherent in the true form.

Watching Larken move through *T'ai Chi* filled River with a sense of loss and longing. To attain such peace and serenity was a goal many people strove for their entire lives. And Larken had found it. How she envied Larken her peace.

The moving meditation ended and Larken again stood still, the ocean waves rioting behind her tall form. River decided she needed to escape before Larken spied her. She tore her gaze away and carefully made her way around the house. Just as she reached the hedge however, and prepared to slip back out onto Greene Street, a hot hand snared her arm.

"So, now I can add spying to your long list of character flaws, I see. Why the devil aren't you at work where you're supposed to be?"

With a gulp of real fear, River lifted her eyes and gazed into the sweaty, angry face of Larken Moore.

CHAPTER THIRTY-ONE

The roar of an airplane passing overhead and the persistent slap of the ocean waves were the only sounds as Larken and River stood in the front yard of Larken's home and regarded one another.

Larken frowned in frustration as she noted the fear shadowing River's eyes. She realized suddenly that River must have been hiding there for some time watching her martial art routine. This was not the first time a person had become uncomfortable with Larken after seeing her in action.

She sighed deeply and abruptly released River's arm to comb fingers through her sweat-dampened hair. She tried to keep her knowledge of the deadly arts a secret but someone, usually someone she cared for, always found out. And their perception of her changed accordingly, due to their lack of knowledge.

"I wouldn't hurt you, River," she said finally, her voice dull and despairing. "You don't understand about these Eastern ways. We learn to fight, to kill, so we won't have to fight and kill. It's almost like a Buddhist koan, an unanswerable riddle which moves in a circular way."

She turned her back so she wouldn't have to face the other's frightened eyes. "Are you familiar with the yin/yang symbol?"

River cleared her throat, trying to find her voice and Larken mentally chastised herself for sneaking up the way she had.

"Yes, of course, positive and negative energy, rebounding on themselves," River said finally.

"Exactly."

Larken paused and fingered the leaves of one of the tall hedges which bordered the Baxter property. "The whole Eastern philosophy incorporates this energy of passiveness and aggression. This time alone is my aggression so my passivity will circle into the outside world."

"Ahh." River's voice sounded excited. "I see. That's how you can be so calm most of the time."

"Yes. And I would never hurt you, never, no matter what you did to me."

River moved closer and laid a delicate hand along the muscles of Larken's back. "I think I believe you. Not an easy task though, after witnessing what you did to that musician and to those things out back."

Larken found herself smiling. River was teasing her and all the anger and fear she'd been harboring dissipated like so much ocean fog. She turned slightly and saw that the fear River's eyes once held had been replaced by amusement...and desire.

She pulled her into her arms and pushed their bodies together with firm force. Her hands tangled in glossy white hair and her lips savored that face, her lips, her eyes. Larken's body, aroused and needy, pressed against River, hips rotating gently. Thoughts of Minorca and infidelity were swept away. The woman was irresistible.

River worried about falling into Larken's arms again for one fleeting instant only. Then Larken's lips found her and she was lost on a tidal wave of passion. She felt herself falling but didn't care and then they were lying in the grass together, Larken's wet, muscled leg thrown over both of hers, and she longed to be naked beside her.

Their kisses were a mingling of breath, of souls, until she felt her body shuddering in surrender. How she wanted Larken! Her hands fluttered about the slim body, trying to pull closer as delicious lips traveled along her neck, seeking entry at the neckline of her shirt. Larken's warm, callused hands crept under the hem of her shirt and moved with sensual slowness along her sides and back, finally surrendering teasing playfulness and roughly cupping one breast.

A hoarse sigh rippled through her as she clutched Larken ever closer, her lips tasting salt and ocean.

"Oh, River," Larken muttered against her neck and River's hands smoothed the tangled cord of tendons in her shoulders. Larken's scent, clean sweat, tempered with heat-smell from the sun and salt from the sea breeze was an inebriating aphrodisiac.

River's eyes fluttered open in surprise at her body's harsh reaction and the unfamiliar surroundings penetrated with a warning. Blue sky amid tree branches jangled that they were not in a private place and some sort of consciousness tried to enter.

"Larken," she gasped weakly, "wait, wait."

Larken lifted her head as if drugged.

"We're outside," River managed to sigh against her ear.

Larken muttered an apology and, pulling River to her feet, they went around the house and up a long wooden stairway outside the building. She caught a glimpse of the wide expanse of ocean before they were inside the shelter of Larken's home.

Within seconds they were in the gloom of the bedroom and Larken lifted River's T-shirt over her head and stood back, the shirt trailing from one hand.

"Ahh, you're too beautiful," she whispered, dropping the shirt to the floor and moving close to caress River's breasts. River's shorts slid away and she was naked. And then so was

Larken and they moved onto the bed, lying side by side, gazing into one another's eyes.

She lifted one hand and unbound Larken's thick, glossy hair, hands stroking gently over heavy, bird-wing brows. She caressed Larken's slim waist, fingertips playing across the thick tautness of her middle.

"I need you, Larken," she whispered against Larken's lips.

Wordlessly, but her soft gaze conveying a world of meaning, Larken rose above her and smoothed their bodies together, her glowing eyes closing at the intense sensation. She cupped the back of River's sleek thigh with her palm as she lifted the leg and wrapped it around her body. River's hands clutched at Larken's firm buttocks as they drove their lower bodies as close to one another as humanly possible. Her hands found Larken's center which rocketed Larken away too soon and she rested her weight diagonally across River, gasping and moaning in delight. She moved then, lower down, and, using hands and tongue, she moved River's body into delicious spasms of cooing madness.

CHAPTER THIRTY-TWO

Reality crept in. River lay tucked into Larken's shoulder, almost asleep, her breath tickling the skin on Larken's chest.

How could she let herself be swept again into River's web of passion? How could she be doing this, sharing this woman with a criminal, a man she practically hated? The thought of River in Minorca's bed gnawed at her but she knew she was helpless to resist. All River had to do was come near her and she melted.

She really had thought she was a woman in control. She knew herself, her needs, her desires, her strengths, and weaknesses, and she had been proud of the early training that had given her this wisdom. But here was River, who, with one girlish, innocent smile, had unraveled all the progress she'd made during the past twenty-five years. She was helpless and she felt somehow diminished.

Bitterly she sought River's body again, her touch bordering on brutality, but after her first initial surprise, River matched her, passion for passion until tenderness crept in and they both slowed into mutual satisfaction.

She gave up then, knowing she was defeated. No matter that Minorca's hated form had occupied this same space, Larken would not be able to turn away. River was like an addiction, some heady drug she was powerless to resist.

When they showered together, later in the afternoon, River noticed that Larken seemed troubled.

"Larken, are you okay about this?"

They were standing together in Larken's spartan bathroom, a cascade of hot water flowing across their flushed, satiated bodies. Larken pulled her from the stream and proceeded to soap her skin gently, hands lingering across every wide expanse of rosy flesh.

"What do you mean?" she responded quietly, delaying.

River turned and caught her gaze so she could understand her fully.

"You seem a little subdued. Is everything all right with you?"

"River," she replied, looking away, "I can't help myself, and there's nothing I can do about it. Let's just...not talk about it, okay?"

She nuzzled River's neck, kissing slowly along her shoulder. River returned the kisses, even as doubt began to sprout in her mind.

CHAPTER THIRTY-THREE

Sylvie, who had been thinking some pretty mean thoughts about River, especially when the huge tour bus stopped in front of the store just at closing, sighed with relief when River returned late that afternoon. She had been forced to call Len in from the back and she wasn't sure whether he was helping or hurting her progress waiting on the customers. River jumped in and soon all customers were dealt with and the store was empty, the front door locked.

"Sylvie, Len," River began when the three of them were finally alone, "I really am sorry I bailed out on you guys today. I am usually not so thoughtless and irresponsible. Can you forgive me?"

Len ducked his head shyly and nodded before disappearing into the back room.

"Hey, it's all right," Sylvie said slowly. "I've had problems myself so I can understand. Did you get everything straightened out?"

To Sylvie's surprise, River burst into tears and threw her arms about the younger girl's shoulders.

"Oh no, don't cry," Sylvie said, rubbing River's back and muttering soothing phrases. "Tell me what's wrong."

"It's so complicated," River replied, backing away and snuffling into a tissue. "Simon wants to marry me and if I don't he'll fire me, and I feel like a failure because the store isn't the way I want it and I'm so attracted to Larken I could die but we have to work together, but we can't because we can't keep our hands off one another. And then she gets mad at me all the time and I can never really seem to do anything right for her. And what kind of a relationship is that anyway?" She paused for air.

Then continued, "But if I marry Simon, I'll have money and I can even open up my own jewelry store one day, which is what I want, of course, but then I'd have to live with him when it's Larken I want. And then there's the mother."

Sylvie was listening to this verbal torrent with patient amazement, but interrupted for clarity, "Whose mother? Larken's?"

River jerked in alarm, "Oh, my gosh, I hadn't thought of that! Larken must have a mother too and I don't even know what she's like. Simon's mother is so beautiful but so cold. She told me to marry Simon even though I don't love him 'cause she didn't love his father. I don't think I want to marry someone I don't love. My mom and dad always talked about the person I would find someday, the great love of my life. If I married Simon I'd be going against everything they have told me all my life. I can't do that."

Sylvie nodded in agreement. "Then will you live with Larken?"

"I don't think she wants to be with me," she wailed, dropping her face onto her folded arms, crying anew. "I don't even think she really l..l..likes me."

"But you said you couldn't keep your hands off one another," Sylvie interjected.

"I know, I know, but that's just desire," River sobbed. "She doesn't *like* me though. She doesn't seem to want to spend real time with me, you know?"

Sylvie nodded as River sobbed on.

Sometime later, River dried her eyes and sat back. Her face was blotched red from weeping but a new determination glowed in her cool blue eyes.

"So, feel better?" Sylvie asked as she gently smoothed hair away from River's forehead.

"I think so. What do *you* think I should do about all this?"

"Well." Sylvie pulled a second stool close and sat next to River so she could hold her hand. "If it was me I would not marry Simon Minorca. That would be a mistake. He's got a lot of money but he also has a real bad reputation around here and you could be getting yourself into the middle of a mess there."

River nodded her agreement, swiping at her swollen face with a fresh tissue.

"Now, Larken, I'm a little confused about," Sylvie continued. "I personally think she's great but I don't know her that well. She's a hard worker, or at least she was until you came along," she said and smiled, trying to cheer the other woman.

"But why doesn't she like me?"

"I think she does. She's just got some kind of hang-up about you, maybe. You say she desires you, right?"

River blushed. "Yeah, in a big way. Both of us are crazy when we get together. I can't figure it out."

"Well, she's gotta respect you too, and like you. Maybe she feels like you don't respect or like her. People can be real funny, especially when it comes to these types of relationships." She rolled her eyes for emphasis. "Believe me, I know. I have friends who are lesbians and they have the same problems everyone else does but often magnified because of the lifestyle."

She paused, her cheeks darkening and her voice lowering. "Try saying no to...you know...for a while. Get to know her in other ways. There's more to life than that."

River dropped her gaze, embarrassed. "You're probably right, Sylvie. I've never been attracted to a woman before, never even thought I would. And then Larken came along and I did just kind of fall into her arms. She's so damned irresistible though and there seems to be some kind of force, a chemistry, I guess, between us."

Sylvie nodded in understanding. "No judgment conveyed, River, I live in a glass house myself and certainly have no right to throw stones. Just try cooling it for a while and see if that works."

"But what about my job? Simon will have me fired if I don't marry him."

Sylvie brushed this away with a grimace of her freckled nose. "Pshaw! Larken wouldn't let him get away with that."

"But he's the money source. If he pulls out we'll have to close this store. I can't be responsible for that." Tears threatened again.

"Look, Larken's no fool. I know for a fact that she and Carter are aware of Minorca's reputation. We've talked about it. If we have to let this store close, then it'll close. *C'est la vie.*"

A sudden, unexpected smile lit River's face and Sylvie leaned back to watch the amazing glow. "You're right, Sylvie. We've just got to fight this thing. I can't believe I was ready to let that snake walk all over top of me. Imagine, me marrying that…that… creep!"

Sylvie tremulously returned River's smile. "So, what are you going to do?"

River sat thinking a moment then answered slowly. "Well, first I think I'll call Larken tonight and have a good long talk with her. Then next week I'm going to come in here and work my butt off, getting everything just the way I want it."

"Is that it?" Sylvie asked when River seemed finished.

"I think I'll practice my *t'ai chi* and maybe even take up *tae kwon do.*"

"What?"

River's welcome laugh rang throughout the empty store as she waved the question aside.

After a moment, Sylvie asked in a worried tone, "What exactly do you plan to change in the store?"

"Oh, don't worry, it's just some organizational stuff I learned in my management courses…"

Her voice faded away as she picked thoughtfully at a hangnail on one of her fingers. "I also need to design more work. I haven't been doing nearly enough."

"I wouldn't worry too much about that," Sylvie reassured her. "Everyone needs a break now and then. Besides, your old designs are still selling like crazy. I sold a bunch of them today. And that opal thing you did, wow! You need to relax, really, and quit beating yourself over the head. Everything is fine."

River took a deep breath and smiled sheepishly. "I sure hope you're right, Sylvie, I do."

CHAPTER THIRTY-FOUR

Larken was waiting for River when she arrived home about six that evening. Her tanned hands held a single sprig of creamy jasmine blossoms that she silently offered as River reached the door to the apartment. The gesture warmed River's heart almost as much as the glow in Larken's eyes.

Nervously River unlocked the door and moved to fetch a shallow bowl for the lovely, fragrant branch. After it was positioned with tender care in the center of her coffee table, she faced Larken, hands wringing in sudden embarrassment.

Larken seemed ill at ease as well. She moved nervously from foot to foot and watching, River realized finally that she had dressed with impeccable care in a rich suit of darkest gray. Her hair was clasped back by barrettes, and, uncharacteristically, a slim watch adorned her left wrist and a signet ring the little finger of her right hand. A mysterious beaded necklace peeked out from the softly rounded bodice of her white shirt. She even smelled especially good, her subtle sandalwood scent permeating the small room.

Larken finally broke the silence, her voice subdued.

"I thought maybe you'd like to go to dinner with me."

It was a simple statement but for River it was full of meaning and her heart sang with joy. Perhaps Larken did want to know her, her mind as well as her body.

Larken shifted uneasily and River realized she was waiting for a response.

"Yes," she barked abruptly, "yes, I'd like that. Let me change." She extended one staying palm as she backed toward her bedroom. "You stay here and...read. There's books on the table there."

She ran into the bedroom and jerked a favorite dress from her closet. She rummaged out a pair of light sandals and, after fetching lingerie from a bureau drawer, she raced into the bathroom for a quick shower.

Larken had been browsing through *Sonnets From The Portuguese*, a book of poems by Elizabeth Barrett Browning, thrilling to the familiar passages of undying love. A small noise behind her drew her attention and she turned.

The words she'd been reading came rushing in a whisper from her lips:

"Thy soul hath snatched up mine, all faint and weak,
And placed it by thee on a golden throne,
And that I love, oh soul, we must be meek,
Is by thee only, whom I love alone."

River was beautiful. She was dressed in a simple off-the-shoulder sheath of darkest red, her platinum hair loose in a shining cloud about her head, her eyes glowing translucent as they softened in reaction to the tender words.

An ache swelled deep within Larken's body and she knew that, whatever happened between them, she would remember this vision of River for the rest of her life.

Rising, she moved to her and cupped her chin in one hand. She pressed her lips to the softness of River's, inhaling deeply of her wonderful scent. River sighed and her arms encircled Larken.

Without warning the kiss deepened and passion flared. Larken cursed herself for moving so close to River. Before all will vanished, she gently moved back and away to hold her at arm's length.

"I made a promise to myself this afternoon. I swore I would learn to control myself when I'm near you, something I've had a hard time with so far, as I guess you know."

River smiled at her indulgently. "I've had the same problem."

Her words sent a new jolt of passion coursing through Larken and she closed her eyes with steely determination. "There are things we need to discuss though. We need to spend time talking."

River laughed her engaging laugh. "I agree, Larken, honey. Let's go to dinner, I'm hungry."

CHAPTER THIRTY-FIVE

Larken's car was sleek and dark gray and impressed River with its neatness and the low healthy thrum of the engine. Larken was an excellent, careful driver and River relaxed into the soft leather seat, her head tilted so she could watch as strong hands and arms guided the vehicle along.

Larken's unusual silence disturbed her at first, until she realized it was only because the men she had dated were full of inane chitchat about themselves and others. Most people feared silence and would chatter on endlessly in an effort to fill the dead air. Silence, on the other hand, seemed to be very much a part of Larken's nature.

Her eyes would find River often, however, her gaze speaking volumes, letting her know she was not forgotten, not for a moment. River returned these glances with intense gazes of her own.

They drove off the island, heading north on the main highway. Blue water shimmered in the dusk on either side of them and, pressing a button, Larken lowered the windows partway.

"Is that okay?" she asked.

River nodded and tilted her face into the gentle ocean wind, savoring the moist, fragrant air as it bathed her cheeks. She was becoming quite fond of Florida.

The restaurant was small and intimate, with no more than ten tables, all of them placed for privacy. The lighting was dim, most of it coming from candles placed on each of the tables. The food was Italian, and homemade bread, rich with fresh butter, was placed before them immediately. After a brief conference, they both ordered and Larken asked their waitress for a wine that turned out to be a delicious blend that flowed like warm honey along her throat.

Gazing across the candlelight at Larken's beautiful, exotic face, River felt as though she'd stepped into a fairy tale where all her fondest wishes were coming true. She found herself waiting for the other shoe to fall, waiting for the bubble to pop; surely something this wonderful could not last forever.

They began talking then and River found the intricacies of Larken's mind fascinating. She told River about life as a military kid, traveling from post to post, all over the world; about how hard it was making new friends all over again at unfamiliar schools.

River, who had lived in the same place since birth, couldn't imagine such a way of life.

"That must have been so uncomfortable for you," she said, laying her hand across Larken's.

Larken covered River's hand with hers. "I became used to it quickly. You come to depend on your family a lot because they're the only familiar faces."

"Do you have a large family?"

"One brother and a sister, both much older than me." She sat back and lifted her wineglass.

"But you were close?"

Larken nodded as she sipped from her glass. "For the most part. Our interests diverged but they both always had my back during the first few weeks in any new school."

River laughed. "We were that way too. Each year our little horde would descend on the school and new teachers were warned to watch out for the Tyler pack. What they did to one, they were told, they'd better be prepared to do to all."

Larken laughed and River thrilled to the sound. "I'd love to meet them, all of them," she said.

River smiled and nodded, feeling shy suddenly. "I'd like that. Maybe you could go back with me during the holidays? To Virginia?"

Larken leaned forward. "It's a date," she whispered, gazing into River's eyes.

River felt her cheeks redden but could not remove her gaze from Larken's. What she saw there enchanted her...warmth, understanding, patience. She could easily imagine a life with this woman. River usually had to guard against trusting too easily but resting this trust in Larken seemed well-placed. Larken, as far as River could tell, possessed a true, honorable spirit and a good heart, a good foundation for any relationship.

The arrival of their dinner distracted them and their talk drifted to Larken's martial art training. She told River about how, as her siblings grew older and moved on, she found herself alone a great deal and she finally had to turn to herself for sustenance, because the pain of parting from friends had proven too great.

She spoke happily about her time in the Far East, especially the time on the tiny island of Okinawa, where she had learned her first karate skills from a master and teacher, Huang Ko, who had taken a forgotten girl-child under his wing. He had taught her how to develop her own personal power within; how to make her life force grow.

Listening to Larken, and questioning the things she did not understand, gave River new insight into this remarkable woman and what had shaped her into the person she was today. She formed a new respect for the martial arts as well, finally understanding the attraction it held for Larken.

During the course of the dinner, her own life in Virginia was explored by Larken and they laughed often as she shared anecdotes of her unusual family. They discussed the men River had cared for and how delightfully strange it was for her to care for a woman in that context.

Larken spoke of deeply loving one woman before, a woman who had hurt her badly, and that she had never been interested in men, partly because she was too dynamic, too threatening to them.

"It's odd, isn't it?" Larken said finally over a dessert of heavy Italian pastry. "We come from such entirely different backgrounds, are so different, yet we seem so very much alike." She paused and her words grew halting, her voice low and embarrassed. "I feel like you are just a missing part of myself. It's like I finally become whole when you are with me."

River watched her uncertainly until she realized Larken was sharing a huge intimacy, how she really *felt*. Her heart soared.

"Larken, I need to tell you something."

Larken stilled, mind filling with dread. She knew River was about to say something about her relationship with Minorca and knew the evening would be ruined by her confession. Her jaw tightened.

"I think I know, River, but please, let's not spoil our evening together. If I have to share, my time will be my time. I can't do it any other way."

River, who was sipping her wine, frowned and swallowed. "What are you talking about?"

"What are you talking about?" Larken countered.

"I just wanted to tell you that I think I'm falling deeply in love with you and I think it's something that's going to last a long, long time. If you have a problem with that, you need to tell me now, and we need to end this before it begins. I can't give this kind of love lightly."

Larken studied her a long beat, looking for deception.

"Do you mean it, River?" she asked finally. "Can you love me only? Can you be faithful to me?"

River smiled and leaned to rest one feather soft palm upon Larken's cheek. "Of course, Larken."

Larken gripped her hand and pressed a lingering kiss to the palm. "You don't know what this means to me, River."

Larken was bubbling with the energy of a child as they left the restaurant.

She drove them to the white beaches of Bahia Honda Key and they sat together on the sand enjoying the slap and hiss of the mighty ocean. They cuddled and talked and Larken told her stories of island folklore, causing River to shiver with horrified delight.

"I want you to have something, River," Larken said finally. "Will you wear it to please me? I want you to see this and think of me when I am away from you next week."

River, who had been leaning against Larken's chest, turned to face her.

"You're going away? Where?"

"I have to buy more opals, remember?" she teased. "I'll only be gone about a week or so."

She reached up and drew the necklace she wore over her head. Moonlight danced on the darkened strand and River wondered at the piece's composition. Larken draped the necklace over River's head and arranged it delicately around her neck.

"It may seem silly to you," she said softly, pulling River against her chest again, "but I believe this necklace has very special power. I wore it for more than ten years while I trained as a martial artist and it is very precious to me. It's the only thing of real value I have to give to you."

River smoothed a fingertip across the beads and when she lifted her eyes, they were filled with unshed tears. "Then I will cherish these beads too, just as I cherish what I feel for you."

She sighed. "I'll miss you so much, though. Please hurry back."

And finally as one day gave way to another, seeking total union, they made gentle, slow love on the beach with only the moon and sea as witness.

CHAPTER THIRTY-SIX

The sun's rays rested hot on River's shoulders as she jogged through quiet downtown streets early the next morning.

She had bid Larken farewell but moments before and her skin still tingled from their closeness. Larken's delicious woodsy scent lingered on her face from the kiss they'd shared with reckless abandon in the parking lot of the apartment complex.

Now, trying to put Larken's absence from her mind, she jogged alone through a mostly sleeping village. The running felt good, her muscles meshing with smooth clarity, the wind passing with easy efficiency in and out of her lungs. She smiled ruefully as she rounded a corner. She'd have to devote a lot more time to running if she ever hoped to match Larken's incredible stamina.

Time passed as River ran. Today was Wednesday, the one day

of the week that Designs by Deidre closed its doors and River could run as long as she pleased. Sweat beaded and ran in tiny rivulets between her breasts and along the small of her back.

Lost in the rhythm of running, it took her several moments to recognize subtle movement behind and to her left. Craning her neck and glancing back, she saw a familiar black limousine cruising the curb alongside.

Simon. Her heart leapt in sudden trepidation.

Slowing her pace, she finally lurched to a walk and turned to face the vehicle.

A tinted window in the back lowered with graceful slowness and Patrice Minorca's face appeared from the dimness.

River breathed a small sigh of relief, glad she didn't have to face Simon just yet.

"Hello," she gasped, wiping a film of sweat from her brow with her palm. "How are you today, Mrs. Minorca?"

"Fine, my dear, just fine." Patrice watched River with cool, impassive eyes. "I'm glad to see you are taking care of your health. You must mind the heat, however, southern Florida heat is tricky and can sneak up on one."

River smiled and playfully shook sweat from her arms and legs. "Tell me about it! I bet I've lost a gallon of water this morning."

"Well, enough exercising then. Come sit with me. I wish to talk with you."

Sudden unreasonable alarm jangled deep in River's being. Why on earth should she be afraid of this elegant woman? Even though she had slyly threatened River's job because River didn't wish to marry Simon, Patrice Minorca had never seemed an ominous figure. And she didn't now, River decided with a nervous laugh. She pushed her misgivings aside and walked slowly around the vehicle.

Tim was by her side in an instant, holding the rear door open.

"Won't I ruin the upholstery?" she asked as she gingerly settled herself onto the leather seat across from the older woman.

Patrice was again dressed with impeccable care, this time in tan linen trousers and a soft silk blouse in a striking mint green color. She appeared sedate and lovely as she reclined against the plush seat. She leaned to remove a white towel from a hidden compartment in the door nearest her.

"Here, dear, dry yourself. Would you like some cold water?"

CHAPTER THIRTY-SEVEN

Across town, at the tiny Key West airport, Larken made ready to board the small commuter plane that would connect her to the Dulles flight that would lift her on her way to Australia. There she would spend a hectic three days gathering beads before flying back to the states and back to River.

The thought of postponing the trip would not leave her mind.

Glancing with worried mien around the small glass-fronted terminal, Larken searched in vain for the cause of her unease. Perhaps it was merely her reluctance to leave River's side. Their time together the night before had been achingly tender, far surpassing any fantasy Larken had harbored about loving someone and being loved in return. No previous relationship had ever given her such passion and such fulfillment. River was her life now and the very idea of going away from her wracked Larken with grief.

"Pull yourself together," she muttered to herself, silently adding, *what will River want with you if you can't even stand on your own two feet?*

Larken had always been fiercely independent and she didn't see that changing now. Except that she really did crave River's company. She enjoyed seeing the day dawn in River's eyes, seeing her pale loveliness each morning, loved feeling her slim heat resting in the bed next to her at night, soft, scented skin smelling of the coconut lotion she smoothed on each evening.

However, there was something else, Larken realized as the nagging feeling persisted, a sense of foreboding. Was River in danger? Was Larken herself in danger? She remembered reading about people who just narrowly missed fatal plane crashes due to a sixth sense, which prevented them from boarding at the last moment. She shook her head with a sigh of perplexity. What should she do? Indecision had suddenly become part of her life. In the past she had always unerringly followed her instincts, had always known the right thing to do. Since meeting River, all bets were off and she was often unsure how to proceed. Was this what true love was all about? This feeling of squirming uncertainty inside when it came to everyday life? The only thing she was certain of anymore was the strong feeling of love she possessed for River.

With another long sigh she tried to dispel her unquiet and leaned to adjust the strap of her bag as the next to last boarding call sounded throughout the tiny airport waiting area. Lifting the satchel, she rose, then hunched and relaxed her shoulders a few times to force her body to relax.

She really did need to go to Australia. Miles Erskin, her contact in that country, had assured Larken on the telephone just yesterday that there were opals waiting, as well as several small, unrefined chunks of gold for which the store had received a special request. Miles was holding several of the precious Harlequin Opals, as well, jet black but with a beautifully patterned design in red and yellow. No one knew about these stones; they were a special, private gift from Larken to River.

Larken was eager to see what River would create from the unusual stones.

But just as she was going through the boarding scanner at security she balked once again. Backing up, she tucked her tall form into a cul-de-sac and let other travelers proceed past.

"Damn!" she muttered, slapping her palm against a nearby support column.

It was at that moment she spotted them and she knew immediately who they were. At first it was the quiet, self-assured air the entire family possessed, moments later it was the familiar white blond hair of the slender, bespectacled man who brought up the ragtag end of the group.

They had obviously just gotten off the latest incoming flight, as they were crossing the tarmac heading into the terminal. Larken quickly moved through the pleasant airport lobby to fall into step beside them. The mother, who looked at Larken with River's eyes, assessed the danger factor of this stranger, then paused and smiled with sweet friendliness.

Larken returned the smile, feeling as if time and space had shifted in some small, subtle way.

The entire group of six people, sensing the mother's hesitation, stopped as one and waited for the stranger to speak. Larken blushed crimson; her mind racing as she wondered how best to proceed. Suppose these people were not who she thought they were?

"I..." she began, only to pause and sigh in embarrassment. "I'm sorry. You no doubt will think I'm crazy, but is your last name Tyler, by any chance?"

"Do we know her, Mama?" whispered a small boy no more than seven years old.

"Well, it looks like we just might," laughed the petite woman as she extended her hand. "Kippy Tyler, and you are?"

"Sorry," Larken gulped as she extended her own hand. "Larken, Larken Moore."

"Ahhh, you work with our River, don't you?" Kippy said with definite recognition. She paused to glance around. "But why are you here to meet us? River wasn't aware we were coming. It was a spur-of-the-moment idea and we didn't call, hoping to surprise her."

"Oh, no, I was flying out myself. To pick up opals in..."

She paused and tried to settle her mind, a mind threatened by how these kind people would react when they discovered their daughter was in love with her. The final boarding call for her flight rang through the terminal behind her.

"Look," she said finally. "Let me take you to River. She's home today."

Kippy eyed Larken with uncertainty. "But weren't you going somewhere?"

Larken smiled ruefully. "I can't. I just have this bad feeling I can't seem to shake." She laughed apologetically. "With my luck it probably means the plane is going to go down."

"Well then, I don't think you should go either," Kippy replied as if the matter were settled. "Obviously you were meant to meet us here and take us to River."

With that, she turned and silently led the group toward the sliding glass doors that opened to the street outside.

"We'd planned on renting a car, Miss Moore," said River's father in a soft, mellow voice. "Could you perhaps guide us to the rental agency."

"Of course," she answered, falling into step beside him. "There's one just around the corner. But, if you like, I can give you a ride in my car."

Both paused in tandem and eyed the four children ranging in age from about seven to fourteen years who were trailing after their tiny mother.

"I hope you have a big car," River's father said doubtfully.

Larken laughed. "Well, maybe not."

"I figured," he agreed, extending his hand. "I'm Alan Tyler, by the way, and it's a pleasure to meet you."

"Likewise," Larken said with a grin as she shook Alan's hand. Walking together, they crossed the parking lot.

CHAPTER THIRTY-EIGHT

"Where are we going?" River asked nervously as the long limousine turned onto a neglected roadway littered with palm fronds and thick green coconuts.

Patrice, smoking with languid grace in a corner of the back, glanced out the window. "I thought I'd show you the house left me by my mother. It's very old but I feel we'll be comfortable there."

"Oh," River replied, sitting back and trying to relax. "I can't stay long, I'm afraid. I have several things I'd planned to do today."

"They can wait, I'm sure," Patrice replied pleasantly. "You and I must talk about poor Simon. You realize he loves you very much, don't you?"

Irritated, River answered with some pique. "We never spoke

about love, Mrs. Minorca. He as much as told me he wanted a decoration to wear on his arm during business gatherings."

"That's just his way, my dear. You know how men are, forever relating to things on a business level, or sports level or whatnot, seldom getting to the heart of the matter. I can assure you he is smitten with you. I have never seen him act so obsessed before."

"He's a big boy now, he'll get over it. I'm afraid I simply cannot marry your son."

Patrice's mouth compressed into a firm line but she did not reply because the limousine had slowed before a large frame house with weathered wooden siding. A huge wrought iron balcony on the second floor dominated the entire front, totally shadowing the wide, Spanish-style front doors. The narrow grounds were mostly unkempt, with wild sea oats and sawgrass predominating. Palms framed the house and a few scrub pines dotted the yard.

Tim opened the door and River reluctantly followed Patrice from the vehicle. Air cooled by the shadow of the close trees flowed across River's sweat-dampened skin and she shivered.

"Come, let's get you into some dry clothing," Patrice clucked maternally. "I keep a full wardrobe here. I'm sure we can find something for you."

"No, really, that's fine," River protested. "I've told you, I really can't stay."

Patrice led the way into a front hall paneled in old, dark wood that had been rubbed to a warm, honeyed sheen. A large staircase led upstairs from just inside the door and Patrice immediately pulled River along these stairs. Tim followed behind bearing a small suitcase. He closed the front door.

Half an hour later River was dressed in a gorgeous India print caftan of softest cotton and still protesting that she had to get home.

Leading the way downstairs, Patrice brought River into a paneled library where hot tea and scones waited on a small table. Nonchalantly, silently, Patrice poured tea into two delicate china cups and handed one to River.

"Look, this has gone far enough," said River angrily, as she returned the cup to the table. "I want to go home. Now."

Patrice sighed and sipped her tea.

"I've brought you here for a reason, River. My son will be here later this evening and I want the two of you to spend some time together, get to know one another. I am sure once you discover what a charming man my son can be you will be more than willing to become his wife."

A sinking feeling swept over River at the other woman's words. She wished desperately she had obeyed her first instincts. She wouldn't be in this dilemma now.

"I'm sorry. That is not possible," she replied firmly. "I've told you before, I will not marry Simon. I am in love with someone else. You'll just have to accept that."

Patrice lit a cigarette and walked to look out a large window, her back to River. "Someone else." She emitted a small bark of laughter. "I've seen your someone else and simply cannot believe you would choose that muscled, army brat woman over my son."

River's eyes widened and her mouth fell open. "Have you actually been *spying* on me?" she asked in disbelief.

"Of course," Patrice answered in a low voice. "You don't think I would allow my son to marry someone I know nothing about, do you? I love him far more than that, I can assure you."

"You've been spying on me," River repeated quietly as if trying to digest the information. "How dare you?"

Patrice sighed and turned to face the younger woman. "Look, marry Simon and you can keep your little woman friend. I'm sure this type of thing has been done before. Besides, what does it matter if it is a man or a woman? A woman is actually better, less of a threat, perhaps."

"You...you bitch!" River cried. She turned abruptly and strode rapidly to the front door. Flinging it open she marched through only to be stayed by a thick muscular arm thrust with impudent force against her chest. An unfamiliar man, a big, burly individual, was standing guard just outside and preventing her escape.

CHAPTER THIRTY-NINE

"I can't imagine where she'd be," Larken muttered apologetically. "I swear I left her here not more than three hours ago."

Kippy Tyler studied Larken, her pale eyes questioning. "She didn't mention any plans she'd made for today?"

"No. No, this was her day off—but she was pretty tired." Larken tried hard not to blush. "She said she was going out for her daily run then coming back home to rest."

They were standing just outside the door of River's apartment. Many minutes of knocking had brought no answer. And they could hear the muted peal of her cell phone from behind the closed door every time they dialed.

Larken was concerned and her sense of foreboding increased. There was no way River would have left her cell if she'd planned to be gone for any length of time.

As if reading her mind, River's teenaged sister, Tide, spoke up. "You don't think anything could have happened to her while she was running, do you?"

Larken faced the young girl squarely, wondering how best to calm the others while dealing with her own galloping fears. "Oh, no, Key West is pretty safe, Tide. Don't start worrying before there's a need to. She's probably just hanging around the library."

"Well, why don't we go get settled in." Alan said finally. "There's a hotel out on the main drag that looks appealing. We'll get a room and see a few sights, enjoy the ocean, then check back here later."

"That's a good idea," Larken said with relief. "Meanwhile, I'll check the library and go see if Beebee has seen her."

Kippy raised one eyebrow. "Beebee?"

"A mutual friend," Larken explained.

After establishing which hotel Alan was referring to, in case she needed to contact him, Larken bid the Tyler family goodbye, her mind clamoring with possibilities. What could have happened to River?

If only this nagging dread would disperse! Larken tried to be reasonable, tried to tell herself that River was still running, that River had gone shopping, even that River was, indeed, at the library. These were all normal activities that River could be expected to do on any given day. She could have forgotten her phone. Why then, this nagging dread? Why was she so worried?

Wearily, with one last lingering look at River's apartment building, she climbed into her car and drove through the streets of downtown Key West, looking for some sign of the woman she loved.

CHAPTER FORTY

River shoved the arm away and again tried to pass. Again the arm stayed her and this time the man moved to stand directly in her path, arms hanging ready at his sides. River backed away uncertainly and realized other men stood at the ready just behind him and over to both sides.

She cried out with indignation and stomped her foot so hard the old wooden boards of the porch floor cracked ominously. Whirling, she strode back into the house to confront Patrice, her chest heaving with anger.

"I can't believe you," she ground out finally. "Don't you know it is against the law to keep someone against their will? You could go to jail for this."

Patrice smiled with cool superiority. "My son owns the jails on this island, my dear River. Do you realize the power he has?

Wouldn't you like to have access to this power? Think what could be yours."

River shook her head vehemently. "Not if it means doing something as despicable as this."

River was becoming more worried with each passing moment. She was entirely in this woman's control and, as far as she knew, no one knew of her whereabouts. Larken was gone, half a world away, and Carter and Sylvie would not even miss her until she didn't show up for work in the morning. Despairing, she felt tears well, but quickly straightened her spine. She would not feel sorry for herself and she would not acquiesce without a fight. She would have nothing to do with Simon Minorca or his family. They could all rot in hell as far as she was concerned.

Lifting her chin, she faced Patrice squarely, her pale eyes darkening with resolve.

Patrice appeared to ignore the threat. She rang a delicate bell on the table that summoned a small, wizened Cuban woman.

"Esa, please take our guest to her room." she turned to River. "Rest now, so you will have a fresh face for my son when he arrives later for dinner. I really am sorry it has to be this way, my dear. If only you had listened to reason at an earlier date, all this could have been avoided."

River watched Patrice with steely eyes. "No, I seriously doubt it. Stupidity has a way of showing itself, no matter how much one tries to gloss it over," she sneered. "You'll regret this day. Moreover, I will not have your son, in any way, shape or form. I despise him and I despise you."

"Well spoken. But I tend to think of a lesbian as a wild bronco, only requiring a disciplining hand to be broken, if you will. My son, a strong, virile man, can certainly change your lifestyle to, shall we say, a more normal one?"

Filled with indignation, River controlled her violent thoughts and quickly followed the tiny woman from the room. There was no reasoning with an unreasonable person.

The room was furnished simply with an antique bed, heavily polished cherry wardrobe, and a marble-topped washstand. A braided, oval rug decorated the center of the floor. Though a lovely room, River's mind refused to focus on the cage in which she had been thrust.

River collapsed on the bed and pondered her options. She needed to collect herself. To make a plan. Escape seemed impossible. Talking sense into Patrice seemed impossible. Perhaps Simon would listen to reason.

She finally allowed tears to wend slow pathways along her flushed cheeks. Simon was probably just as guilty as his obsessive mother. They, no doubt, plotted River's abduction together. Why had she ever gotten into that car? She should have known better. If she ever saw her mother again she would tell her it wasn't only strangers in cars who posed a threat.

Weeping quietly, River detached her keys from the loop around the strap of the sandals Patrice had given her to wear. How normal her life had been when she had used these keys. One opened her apartment, two opened the doors of Designs by Deidre, and one opened the door to her parents' home in Virginia. The last key, dented and scratched, fit the ignition of the old Toyota truck that she drove while at home.

Clutching the keys to her chest with one hand and the necklace she wore, the one Larken had given her, with the other, using both as talismans to ward off evil, River summoned Larken's beautiful face to her mind and relived their time together. She remained, slumped and motionless, as day turned into dusk.

CHAPTER FORTY-ONE

River roused when she heard voices in the hall outside. With eyes smarting from despair, she watched the closed door, trying to make out who was talking.

It sounded like Patrice, but she was speaking in a fast, urgent tone, her words pleading. After a moment she was interrupted by a loud male voice and River recognized it immediately. Simon.

The two, mother and son, appeared to be arguing and River supposed the altercation concerned her abduction. Perhaps Simon would let her go now. Her heart lifted in sudden hope. Simon was no fool and surely he was aware that keeping her a prisoner was a ridiculous, foolhardy idea.

Rising, she smoothed her dress down, just as the huge wooden door swung open.

"River, my love, please forgive mother this indiscretion,"

Simon said, rushing to her side. "I assure you, she acted out of love for us both."

"Love? You call this love?" River found her voice finally and though starting out weak, the volume soon escalated, until it was a wail of indignation. "I am coerced into coming here, treated like a common prisoner and you want me to forgive her?"

Simon's manicured hands fluttered with unfamiliar helplessness. "But River, she meant no harm, really."

River, no longer caring enough to dispute the man, swept past Simon and rushed to the open door. She rudely pushed Patrice to one side and fled along the plush, carpeted hallway. But the effort was again futile; a tall man in a business suit stopped her with his broad body just as she reached the wide staircase.

Screeching her indignation, River beat at his chest with both fists. "You can't keep me here, you can't! This is not the Middle Ages! People just don't kidnap other people!"

Simon was behind her then, his voice low in her ear. "Please, my love, let's talk about this. Mother has arranged a wonderful dinner for the three of us. The least we could do is refresh ourselves with some food and then look at this problem with new eyes."

Tears bloomed in River's eyes and a wave of hopeless despair snatched her up. "I can't eat," she muttered. "I can't."

"Certainly you can eat. Come now, you're only upsetting yourself. A beautiful woman such as yourself should have only smiles and laughter in her life."

Slowly Simon began leading her downstairs, the guard falling into line behind them.

"Are you coming, Mother?" Simon called over his shoulder. "Please don't delay, I'm sure we are all famished."

Pure hatred grew in River as Simon seated her at the table then rushed to hold his mother's chair. Patrice kept her gaze averted until Simon was seated, then she glanced up at him. The look of love and devotion she favored on her son gave River pause. It was obvious now that Patrice lived her life entirely for her son; he was her world. It was little wonder then that she would do such a thing as deprive another human of her freedom, if she thought that was what her son wanted more than anything else.

This realization did little to change River's current dilemma.

"Please Simon," she began. Pausing to clear her throat she resumed, her voice pleading but calm. "You must realize you can't keep me here. I have commitments, a job, a life. I certainly can't stay here."

With nervous, staccato gestures, Patrice lit a cigarette. "It's only for a short while, River. Just so you can make a fair assessment of Simon. How can you know him as the good man he is if you are apart all the time?"

"I don't care what a good man he is," protested River hotly. "I've told you, I will not marry your son."

She turned to Simon and gestured weakly. "It's not that I dislike you, although I must say this little escapade has not helped you any. I just cannot care for you the way she wishes me to."

Simon sipped his wine and nodded as Esa stepped in with a tray of salads. He politely waited for her to serve the food and quit the room before speaking. "I understand, River, really I do, and, if it were left up to me, I would set back the clock to a time before this unpleasantness. Please realize that."

"You can," River replied vehemently, her hand striking the table so hard silverware rattled against china. "Just open the door and let me walk through it."

Simon smiled a sickly smile. "Alas, that's something I can't do as yet."

"Why? Tell me a good reason why."

Simon's face was grim and River was able to see suddenly who he really was, not just the kind, generous man he presented to the world. She saw his true face, the face of a man who held infinite power over his environment. A man who had killed to gain that control. River glanced at Patrice and realized there was actual fear beneath that veneer of love and devotion.

"Why, Simon?" she repeated weakly.

For long agonizing minutes he picked at his salad as if examining each lettuce leaf for infestation.

"You could cause me a great deal of harm, my love. My dear mother has unwittingly set into motion a chain of events that could prove harmful to the lot of us."

Patrice made as if to protest this but he silenced her with a curt wave of his hand. "I know she acted out of love for me, that is not in question. The result is simply this: I cannot allow you to leave because you would go to the authorities and tell them what has happened."

River's relief exploded in a short laugh. "Then allow me to go. I swear to you I will not tell anyone about what has happened. Just let me go home and all will be forgotten. I swear, really."

Simon smiled as if the most genial host in the world but his dark eyes were very cold. "Kidnapping has such an ugly penance. The FBI is brought in, investigations launched. Very nasty."

"But I've told you I will not tell!" Why wouldn't he believe her?

"I know, my dear. You would try to abide by your guarantee but I am a very wealthy, powerful man. I did not become this way by taking chances on anything. If a chance must be taken, it is a small risk, very small. Now, to insure the odds, I suppose we could say, I feel you and I should be married. Just as soon as possible, so your incarceration can end. As you probably know, if we are married, you are no longer a risk to me or anyone else connected with me."

"But..." River was stunned. "I can't marry you. I...I don't love you."

"No matter." He waved his hand nonchalantly, his lips downturned. "You will grow to be fond of me."

"But I love someone else!" she blurted.

Simon's interest was piqued and he sat forward, carefully placing his elbows on the tablecloth. "Someone else? Who is he?"

River dropped her eyes. "I can't tell you that."

"I can," Patrice volunteered, ignoring the angry glare River directed toward her.

He turned to his mother. "And what do you know about all this?"

"I know her lover is a woman. River's a lesbian."

Simon inspected River with glowing, speculative eyes. "No she's not," he said after many moments had passed. "This body was made for a man's touch. I have no doubt of that. It was certainly not meant to be wasted on another woman."

River's mouth dropped open in awed indignation. "I beg your pardon. What the hell do you know about my body and what it is meant for? You don't even know who I really am and you have gall acting as if you do!"

Patrice chuckled suddenly, drawing River's attention. "Any man, especially one as virile as my son, would feel threatened by your preference, River, my dear. Surely you understand. Please don't make matters worse for yourself."

"Matters worse!" River repeated. "Look here 'my dear,' it can only get better as far as I'm concerned. If there is a hell on earth, I've certainly found it. This has to be rock bottom."

"So tell me more about this lover of yours. Do I know her?" Simon was clearly intrigued.

River studied him with cold, hawk-like eyes. "I won't tell you anything."

He sighed and leaned back in his chair. "I have no objection to you keeping this...lover, as long as it is someone I approve. See how easy I am to get along with, dear River? How many husbands would let their wives keep their female love interests? I can assure you, you will be happy as my wife."

River stood on shaky legs, unable to endure any more of this insanity. "That I'll never know, sir, that I'll never know."

She glanced around the elegant table. Patrice sat with head bowed, her cigarette sending up a vertical plume of soft gray smoke. Simon watched River with angry, determined eyes.

"I'm sorry," she said after a few seconds. "I feel ill. I'm going to bed."

Turning, she walked unsteadily from the dining room and into the front hall. One of Simon's men still stood guard at the front door, another at the first landing of the staircase.

With a sigh she ascended, ignoring the guard on the landing as she brushed past him. Gaining her room, she found another guard stationed just outside the door. As he had pointed out, Simon was a man who left little to chance.

Closeted safely in her room, with the door locked from her side, River gave her tears free rein. Crying quietly, her heart heavy with fear and despair, she crossed to the window and peered out into the gathering dusk. A tall man, another guard, stepped into the glow from an outside light. His head bowed and cocked to one side as he lit a cigarette, then he looked up at the window. Seeing her there, he straightened and smiled, waving the hand that held the red, fiery dot of his cigarette.

River stepped from the window and snatched the draperies together. Damn Simon and his men!

But the sudden flash of fire as the man lit his cigarette had given River an idea. Perhaps she could set the house afire and escape in the pandemonium the blaze would cause.

She sat on the side of the bed and wrapped one arm about the tall end post. How would she do it? She fingered the bedspread. Would it burn?

Then she remembered. She had no way of setting a fire, no matches, no lighter. If only her room had been fitted with a fireplace, such as those many of the homes back in Virginia possessed, she might have found matches. Key West was seldom cold, so there was no need for a fireplace.

After a cursory, unsuccessful search of the room, she sat on the edge of the bed and tried to think of some possible loophole Simon had missed, some mistake that would allow her to escape. She decided finally to try and obtain a lighter or matches the next morning at breakfast. After all, at least one person in this household smoked, there had to be something left lying about.

Thus resolved she finally drifted off into fitful sleep, thoughts of Larken comforting her.

Sometime during the night she roused as the door to her room was tried. She pulled the bedspread tighter about herself as Simon whispered her name. Thankfully, the door was bolted from the inside and he finally went away. River spent the rest of the night trembling in fear, trying to decide which of the room's furnishings she could use as a weapon if he came back and forced the door.

CHAPTER FORTY-TWO

The next morning, just before daybreak, Larken approached the employee entrance of Designs by Deidre. River had not answered repeated phone calls the night before and, at four a.m., when Larken visited the apartment, all had been quiet and still, no lights shining from the windows and no answer to Larken's knock.

She flashed back to Deidre's disappearance and horror nibbled at her heart.

There was no sign of her at the store either and Larken's heart felt as though it would stop beating. She tried to calm herself and think seriously about working but found it impossible. She tried to sit idle and force all thought from her mind but found that impossible as well.

River's parents stopped by shortly after the store opened

for business and Larken hated the alarm that blossomed in their faces when she, once again, had to inform them that she had not seen or been contacted by River. They stayed at the store, nervously sipping tea in the back room as they waited for something, anything.

Carter came in about ten and Sylvie silently brought her over to Larken.

"What's going on? Is it River?" Carter's concern etched her features. "Is everything all right? Is she sick?"

Larken took a deep breath and began talking. She told Carter about River going off to run, about her family arriving, about checking at the apartment, about River not showing up for work.

Throughout the narrative, Larken could sense Carter's agitation increasing but there was nothing she could do to allay the other's fear.

"Oh, no, Larken. It's like Dee all over again. I just can't… You've tried everything you can think of, right?" Carter asked sharply.

"Yes, I haven't called the police yet. I did try the hospital. And I've checked locally. No one has seen her."

"Contacting the police is probably a waste of time," Carter said quietly. "We'll keep in touch with the locals and put out the word, you know how news travels here." She paused and indicated the Tyler clan. "Her family, right?"

Larken nodded. "Yes. We're all just kind of waiting for her to show up."

"Oh, Jesus," Carter said, sighing. "Larken, you know River. We've known her for many weeks now. She is not irresponsible. She's never late unless she has a damned good reason and she certainly would not disappear like this without giving those close to her a detailed itinerary. I've got to be honest and tell you this doesn't look good. So we need to work hard, Larken, we need to find her."

Larken introduced Carter to the Tyler family but she was numb. Carter's words had paralyzed her. Something was terribly wrong.

Kippy paled considerably as she talked with Carter. She

made notes on a memo pad kept by the phone and Larken heard the name of Key West's chief of police, the name and location of the closest clinic, as well as that of a local investigator. The name of the investigator sparked Larken's mind into action and with a hurried farewell, she raced from the store.

Twenty minutes later Larken was on Plantation Key talking to Johosh.

"I don't know, Larken. I haven't worked a real case for more than two years. My contacts are rusty. You sure you want to trust me with this one? You might be better off getting someone more recent." His broad Native American face was somber.

"Jo, you know more than these new people ever will. That's it. I trust you to find her for me."

Johosh studied Larken's exhausted, terrified countenance. "You really love her, don't you?"

"Yeah," Larken admitted, her anguished green eyes seeking understanding and acceptance in Johosh's gaze. "More than I ever thought possible. I think I'll die if we don't find her soon."

Johosh nodded and looked away, speaking with wisdom. "You won't die, but you may wish you could. Now, tell me everything you know."

CHAPTER FORTY-THREE

River woke the next morning with new resolve. She knew she had to be strong and cunning if she wanted her life to return to normal. The Minorca family had no right to dictate the path her life would take and, upon reflection, the thought that they were trying to filled her with quiet fury.

The small bathroom adjoining her room was well stocked with soap, shampoo and other toiletries, even a new toothbrush, so she took the opportunity for a refreshing, energizing shower. The bureau and wardrobe held an adequate quantity of clothing, even though they certainly belonged to Patrice. With a grimace of distaste, River chose and donned dark cotton trousers and a white sleeveless knit shirt. She hated the boar bristle brush provided so she combed fingers through her tousled platinum strands. Looking in the full-length mirror, River felt much better than she had the day before. She had restored a certain measure of control to her life and felt imbued with new confidence for the battle ahead.

A guard was still posted outside her door but he allowed her to pass unmolested, as did the guard at the bottom of the stairs. She stepped into the dining room and found Patrice seated at the heavy antique table, a steaming pot of coffee before her.

"Ahh, River. I trust you slept well," she said with genteel good humor as she looked up at her.

"Cut the niceties, Patrice. Don't pretend to like me and I won't pretend to like you, okay?" River seated herself at the table and reached for the pitcher of orange juice.

Patrice appeared hurt. "But River, I do like you. Why do you think I went to all this trouble?"

"You went to all this 'trouble,' as you call it, just to win brownie points with your son. It has nothing to do with me, really."

The older woman's expression hardened. "Being belligerent to me won't help you get away, you know."

"Just what *will* help me get away? Can you tell me that?" River reached for a muffin.

Patrice shrugged. "Nothing, I'm afraid. Simon has his mind made up. The wedding is set for tomorrow at noon."

River choked on her food. "What?"

Patrice allowed a victorious smile to curve her lips. "Yes, soon we shall be one happy family."

"Like hell we will," muttered River. "I'm not marrying your son. I've told you that and I mean it."

Patrice chuckled and lit a cigarette. "You will, my dear, so you might as well prepare yourself."

River didn't answer; her eyes were too busy following the gold-plated lighter Patrice had used to light her cigarette. Chewing her muffin, she watched as the lighter was secreted into a special pocket in Patrice's gold cigarette case. Dismay filled her.

She permitted her eyes to roam about the sun-filled dining room, studying the smallest details. The house overall was furnished simply, obviously a second home, so other than the usual lamps, ashtrays and the occasional artwork or photo, there was very little surface clutter. Eagerly, her gaze sought the serving table that bore several silver-domed serving platters and a silver chafing dish. Her gaze fastened on the chafing dish.

Patrice was watching so she lowered her eyes.

"These are good muffins. Did Esa make them?"

Patrice nodded and sipped from her cup. "Yes, she's a marvelous cook. She's been with our family for many years, since before my mother's death."

"How did your mother die?"

"Natural causes. She lived to be eighty-seven."

"Were these things hers?" River gestured toward the serving sideboard with its weight of silver.

"Oh yes, I've left things very much like they were. Perhaps you and Simon would like to honeymoon here. It's very cozy. Simon plans on taking you away—one of those godawful barbaric places, I suppose, Brazil or the like. I think you'd be much happier here."

River frowned but decided not to argue with the woman. Instead she rose to her feet and crossed to the sideboard. "Mind if I look at these? They really are lovely."

"Yes, go ahead," Patrice agreed, lifting the social register of the local paper.

River moved slowly along the line of serving dishes, running her fingers lightly over the cool, polished silver. At the chafing dish, she paused, offered a silent prayer that Patrice was not watching, and slid her fingers beneath the convex bottom of the dish. Luck was with her; a small book of matches had been stored with the chafing dish, to light it the next time it was needed.

With slow, careful movements, she tucked the folded book of matches into the wide waistband of the trousers she wore, her other hand still caressing silver. Making sure the matches were completely hidden she turned back to the table and returned to her seat. Patrice continued to peruse the newspaper, her head tilted delicately to one side.

CHAPTER FORTY-FOUR

Simon Minorca strode into the showroom of Designs by Deidre with his men following closely.

"Carter, what's wrong? I came as soon as I could after getting your message. Has something happened?"

Carter stepped from behind the counter, her face grim. "I hate to be the one to tell you this, Simon, but River has disappeared."

"Disappeared? Disappeared, how?" He gave Carter a direct, accusatory stare.

Carter dropped her eyes. "We don't know. She left to go jogging and has been missin' ever since."

Larken stepped from the back room, pausing in surprise as she saw the man whose large presence filled the showroom. Alan trailed behind her.

"This is River's father," said Carter to Simon. "Alan Tyler, Simon Minorca."

The two men shook hands and Larken noted the tightness of Minorca's smile.

"I can assure you, Mr. Tyler, no expense will be spared in locating your daughter. I will see to that personally. Have you checked with whoever saw her last?"

"That would be me," volunteered Larken. "I saw her in the morning before she left to go running." She hid her dislike of the posturing man before her.

"And she didn't say anything? Didn't tell you her plans?" Simon's expression was one of disbelief. He was watching Larken with glistening, keen eyes.

Larken stiffened and her voice was clipped. "No. She did leave me with the impression she would be returning to her apartment after her run."

Simon moved to stand by the glass door and look outside. "And just what were you doing with her that early yesterday, on her day off?"

Larken's eyes widened but she maintained her stoic calm. "Is that really any of your business?"

"It could be," he answered, turning his cold eyes on her. "Especially if foul play is involved. You were the last person to see her and I understand from the staff here that you two did not exactly hit it off when River came to take over the store. Did you argue that morning?"

Larken smiled; an expression that seemed to take Minorca aback. "No, we didn't argue. We talked like two mature adults. I have no problem with River and she has none with me, okay? And I certainly didn't harm her in any way. That's not *my* style." Her tone clearly implied that it might be his.

Minorca glared at Larken a moment before regaining his bland smile of social ambiguity. "Quite right. I am so distressed, I don't know what I am saying. Forgive my suspicions."

Larken inclined her head. "Of course."

Turning to Alan, Minorca quickly ascertained what had been done to locate River and what was left still to do. Alan had called the clinics on the islands as well as the hospitals on the mainland. No one fitting River's description had been admitted or even examined in the past two days. The only unidentified body, brought in from the Miami area, had turned out to be African-American.

Minorca paced with impatient energy. "Then what's left to do? I think I will employ a private investigator. That may take more time than we wish to spend but I see no other avenue to take. How do you feel about this, Alan?"

Alan looked at his wife but finally shrugged shoulders heavy with grief. "I just want my River back, safe and sound if possible. Whatever it takes."

"Good. I'll let you know as soon as I hear something." He handed Alan a business card. "Call me here if you receive any news, no matter how trivial. I too, care very much for your daughter. She is a lovely human being and, in fact..." He paused for effect. "I have asked her to be my bride."

A sudden silence fell after Minorca swept from the store.

"Whoosh!" said Sylvie. "Why do I always feel as if I've been struck by a tornado after he's passed through? River won't marry him, will she?"

Larken sneered at the glass walls fronting the showroom as she watched Minorca step into his long black car.

"I hope not. And it's power, Syl, simple power. That man has it. But he's stupid."

"Stupid, how?" Alan asked.

"I've never thought of Simon as stupid, Larken. He's worth a fortune, you know," Carter interjected.

"Yes, I realize that. And his money is what makes him invincible, or so he thinks."

"Larken, please stop talking in riddles. I can't think today," Carter pleaded, holding her head dramatically.

Larken smiled at her. "I know where River is."

Alan pushed forward to study Larken's face. "Where?"

"Minorca has her. He asked why I was with her yesterday on her day off. Not one of us mentioned *when* she disappeared, now did we? For all he knew it could have been this morning."

"By God, she's got something!" Sylvie said.

Carter pondered this new information before lifting an

angry face. "And I didn't tell him either. That snake! What the hell is he up to?"

"Well, let's go get her," said Alan. "Do you know where he lives?"

Larken turned to face the others. "Look, we can't just go busting in there. Minorca is very powerful and, I'm inclined to believe, dangerous. A close friend, a former private eye, is helping me locate River. I'm going to call him and tell him this latest development. My question is this: will you trust us to find out where River is? And what the situation is?"

She turned away to hide eyes that were abruptly filling with tears. "Suppose she wants to be there? Has anyone thought of that?"

Silence fell as they mulled the idea over.

"Nope, River would have told someone. And why would Minorca go through this charade? She's close to her mother, to all of us. One of us would have known something about this if she had gone of her own free will." Alan stated all this firmly.

"Also, she would not have abandoned the shop that way. Not without someone to cover for her. She knew I was only a phone call away, and could have been here to help mind the store if she was going to be away," scoffed Carter.

"I agree," added Sylvie. "She always tells me when she has to leave early or anything like that. She's so careful about it. I can't see her just running off."

Larken took a deep breath and tried to quiet her jealous fears. "Yeah, well, you guys just hang here and I'll see what I can do. I need to make a call."

She disappeared into the back room and Alan, Carter and Sylvie stared helplessly at one another.

CHAPTER FORTY-FIVE

Three hours later Johosh and Larken sat in the Native American's dented Ford pickup truck and watched the Minorca home through binoculars.

"I tell you, she's not there," said Johosh with conviction. "There's no more tension here than what is normal for a typical Mafia Don. The cleaning ladies are still cleaning, gardeners still working. And look, there's a skeleton guard up. There'd be more to keep a captive."

"I respect your instincts, Jo, but you've got to respect mine. I tell you, Minorca knew too much. He has to be involved."

"Then he's got her somewhere else, is all I can say. She's not here." Johosh sounded angry.

"Hey, chill," Larken said, laying a comforting hand on his forearm. "What's really bothering you?"

"I just got bad feelings about this."

Larken's heart lurched. "What do you mean." She studied his face, eyes moving rapidly.

Johosh shrugged. "I can't stand sitting here wasting time. We need to find her."

"What did that truck mean earlier? The truck that had you so interested, catering, or something."

"Yeah, I can't quite figure that one out. He's planning something..." He broke off as a truck rumbled past their sheltered hiding place.

The truck, bearing the logo Island Fashions, with the cursive addendum *for the perfect wedding* paused before the front door of the Minorca home.

"Well," sighed Johosh. "That answers a lot."

"What do you mean?"

"Obviously there's going to be a wedding." His eyes sought out Larken's. "I'm really sorry. I was afraid of this."

Larken looked away, studying one of the hands lying limply in her lap. "No, she loves me, Jo. I know she does."

"Look, Larken, it's real easy to say that but...you know that kind of life can be hard. Look what happened before with that other woman you had."

"Don't remind me of that, old man. I don't need help to remember," Larken growled through gritted teeth.

"Well, face facts then. This idiot has money. He's polished as hell, and has doors open for him all up and down the coast. That's mighty tempting to a young bird like this one."

"Bullshit," Larken snapped, reluctant to admit her own thoughts had flown in the same direction.

Johosh suddenly rose in his seat and peered through the binoculars. "Look, there he goes."

Several of Minorca's men led the way out the front door, one carrying what appeared to be a large clothing box. Minorca followed, dressed with impeccable care in a tailored blue suit, his hair smoothed into its usual ponytail. The entire contingent got into two cars and they moved out along the driveway, right past the grove of palms that hid the dark blue Ford truck with Larken and Johosh crouched below the dashboard.

Following Minorca proved difficult due to island logistics; any following vehicle was easily spotted if it stayed with one too long. Johosh held well back though, trusting instinct and keen vision. Heading north along the island's quiet, tree-shaded streets, they finally emerged onto Venetian Drive and headed into the salt flats lying behind the airport.

"Where the devil are they going," muttered Johosh as he kept the dark tail of the limousine just in view on the turning stretch of road before them. Crossing over onto Airport Boulevard, the limousine turned into a neglected road and slowed perceptibly.

"I can't follow any further," said Johosh. "I'm going to pull off here so they won't spot us. How's your wind today? You up for some cross-country?"

Larken eyed him doubtfully. "I'm good, but what about you...your leg?"

Johosh took a deep breath. "We'll take it easy. I'll be fine."

"Well, we didn't come this far for nothing," Larken said with a sigh. "Lead on, big brother. I'm right behind you."

Johosh parked the truck behind a cluster of decrepit outbuildings and fetched his gun from its home strapped to the inside of the truck's sun visor.

"I'm ready, let's hit it," he said.

Following the Minorca limousines on foot, the two trotted along the side of the road, ducking into the lush, razor-sharp scrub brush as much as possible so they wouldn't be spotted.

CHAPTER FORTY-SIX

River was very much a pacifist by nature and about as far from destructive as a person could get, even hating to disturb a sleeping cat. So setting fire to the home of Patrice Minorca's late mother was proving harder than expected. She fancied she could see the frowning face of the old woman in every corner of her bedroom.

"Look, I'm sorry lady, but I just can't stay here and marry your grandson. I'd rather die."

She realized that even if her plan backfired and she was trapped and consumed by the flames, that resultant fate would be better than having to endure Simon's hated hands on her flesh and trying to live life as his showpiece. Something like that would not be bearable after knowing Larken's love.

"Oh, Larken," she sighed, "why did you have to go away just now?"

Her hands felt for the necklace Larken had given her their last night together on the beach and she felt comforted by its smooth warmth. Pulling the strand into the light, she examined the stones for the hundredth time; small ovals of jade. Obviously hand-carved, the beads were so old that most of the carved texture had worn away. Because the beads ranged in color from dark to light green, to an intriguing lilac color, River knew the stones were very rare—true Chinese jade as opposed to the more common nephrite.

She could only speculate on the necklace's origins and would have loved to hear its history from Larken if things had turned out differently. Tears swelled and threatened to spill but River blinked them away. She had to remain strong. The thought of never seeing Larken again...of not being able to say a final goodbye...was torturing her.

She shook herself mentally. She would see Larken again. She would lie beside Larken again. Studying the beads, she found one the exact shade of Larken's eyes when they were darkened by passion. Tenderly she kissed the bead, imagining Larken's spirit within.

"Soon, love," she whispered, tucking the necklace back into the opening of her shirt. She pulled the book of matches from her waistband and surveyed the room to find the most flammable object, eventually choosing the sheers from the window drapes. Using a wad of tissue from the bathroom, she piled it beneath the window drapes and knelt to strike a match.

Excited voices sounded in the hallway and River noted with dismay that she had neglected to bolt the door. Reluctantly, but quickly, she shoved the matches and the pile of tissue beneath the drapes, between fabric and wall, and leapt to her feet. And just in time, for seconds later a knock sounded at the portal to her room.

"River, it's Patrice. See what Simon has brought you!"

The door swung wide and Patrice entered with a trio of Cuban women juggling a large box and a small suitcase amongst themselves. The box was placed on the bed and the women crowded around River.

"Well, open it," Patrice urged. "Let's see what it is!"

"You go ahead," River replied, absently beckoning toward the gift.

With a frown of disapproval and a chiding glance, Patrice complied, lifting out an enormous froth of white lace and silky white satin.

The Cuban women began chattering among themselves and Patrice studied the frock with a practiced, greedy gaze. "He thinks much of you, my dear," she said softly to River. "Enjoy this time, this treatment, and keep his interest strong so it will continue."

"I don't want it," River said, stubbornly setting her delicate chin into a firm line. "How many times must I say it —I will not marry your son!"

"Look at this, you fool," Patrice hissed, shoving the dress into River's face. Hard stones hit her brow and lips and she realized there were sparkling diamonds sewn into the lace. Seed pearls adorned the satin and the wide skirt and train were embroidered with diamonds in a pale blue color.

"Shit," River muttered, knowing the dress started at ten thousand dollars. If Simon could spend that on a wedding dress, then there was no limit to his power.

"Well, some reaction, you ungrateful bitch," Patrice scolded, laying the dress carefully across the bed.

"Is there a problem?" asked Simon.

River and Patrice whirled in unison to see him standing in the doorway, shoulder supported by one jamb. He appeared relaxed and confident and River felt even more anger stir in her gut.

"When are you going to stop this nonsense, Simon? I am not marrying you tomorrow or any other day. You might as well shoot me or stab me or whatever it is you do to people who you think will talk. I'll have none of this and I mean it. You can just take your fancy dress back to wherever you got it from and get a refund because I'm not wearing it." Her breathing was rapid and a deep flush had appeared high on each cheek as she vented.

Simon threw back his head and laughed aloud. "A refund! Isn't she precious, Mother? So innocent, but so feisty. A baby tiger ready to brawl with nothing but her baby teeth."

Esa entered, bearing a heavy tumbler with pale amber liquid inside. She crossed to River and offered it with bowed head.

"What's this?" River queried the room full of people in general. "I didn't ask for this."

"Of course you didn't, River. A good host always offers refreshment. Please drink it, it won't hurt you. It's fine scotch, aged for many years. A favorite of mine." He lifted his own glass in a silent toast.

River cast a jaundiced expression upon her tormentor but took the drink as Esa backed respectfully from the room. She didn't much care for the smoky taste of scotch but felt the need for fortification if she was to go ahead with her plan. If these fools ever left her alone again.

She turned away and sipped delicately from the glass. It was good, surprisingly good, so she sat on the bed and sipped, ignoring Simon and Patrice as they talked about the dress and how well it was made.

She studied the dress from a distance, not much liking the Victorian cut of the bodice or the pegleg sleeves. The diamonds and pearls imparted a lovely sheen but other than that, the dress had little merit as far as she was concerned. Oh, would this gathering of people never leave and let her be at peace?

She gulped the last of the scotch and steadied herself as the room began to spin. She remembered then that she had not eaten much during the past forty-eight hours. Standing unsteadily, she carried the glass to the bureau and carefully placed it atop it. Simon caught her as her knees buckled and she heard their voices as if from very far away.

"It will be all right now, Mother. She'll go along obligingly with whatever we bid her do. This drug allows her to remain conscious but robs her of her will to resist. Wonderful stuff."

Patrice helped her son lift River onto the bed, carefully pushing the dress aside. "Why haven't we been using this all along then?"

"It's toxic if used for too long. We'll just use it until after the ceremony tomorrow then let her body sweat it out after that," Simon said patiently.

"But will she be okay for the wedding? She won't embarrass

us, will she? I couldn't face my friends again if she came to her senses and began berating the lot of us during the ceremony."

"I've taken care of that, as well. I've arranged that the ceremony itself will be private, citing a shy bride as my reason. All the guests will be at the reception and River will appear once briefly, then disappear again because she is shy. See? Easy as pie."

River heard the dress rustle once more as darkness fluttered at the edges of her mind.

"Shame to waste such a beautiful dress on a private ceremony and one small appearance. I don't understand why she won't see reason and seek to be your wife," Patrice complained. "Foolish girl."

"I bought the dress for River, Mother, not so everyone else could drool over it. She will always have the best I can offer, no matter whether others see it or not."

Patrice's voice was warm and it echoed through River's head as darkness descended. "You will be such a good husband, Simon. I envy River her good fortune."

CHAPTER FORTY-SEVEN

"I say we go now," Larken whispered close to Johosh's left ear.

"No," Johosh whispered back, chopping his hand downward to emphasize the negative. "There's too many of them. It's suicide."

Mosquitoes buzzed about their heads with annoying intensity as Larken and Johosh crouched behind a high stand of sea laurel. Scraping sawgrass tufts met their every move and Larken felt as though she would scream if she didn't get somewhere else soon.

The unfamiliar house Minorca had entered was visible through the dusk because of its many outside lights and, utilizing binoculars, Johosh witnessed several things that confused him. There were guards posted at irregular intervals all around the perimeter of the grounds as well as at each entrance. Why did

Minorca need so much security? Was he really holding River here against her will?

"I don't know about this, little sister. I'm not sure your lady love wants to be here."

Larken swatted a mosquito. "You're not? Why?"

"Too many guards. Either Minorca is afraid she'll try and get away or else he's expecting Fellowship action."

"Christ, that's all we need, to fall into the middle of a Don war," Larken murmured with disgust. Something slithered along her right sneaker and she had to stifle a cry as she lunged backward. Her sudden movement sent a resting bird into flight.

"Will you be quiet," Johosh scolded in a stage whisper. "You'll get us caught yet."

They sat still as two stones until they were sure their hiding place was secure, then Johosh leaned toward Larken.

"You stay here and watch through the binoculars. I'm going to go closer and see if I can figure out exactly what's going on in there. I'll be back as soon as I can and we'll decide our next move."

Larken grabbed his arm as he rose. "Be careful. Those goons look rough."

Johosh smiled and gave her a thumbs-up gesture. He crept silently into the night.

Larken waited.

CHAPTER FORTY-EIGHT

River was alone. The drug Simon had given her made her limbs feel heavy and useless. She moved a thick, swollen tongue around in her mouth trying to moisten the cavity. It did little good, she still felt as though she had a mouthful of sawdust.

Trying to be as quiet as possible, she allowed her body to slide off the side of the bed, hitting the floor with ill grace. She lay panting, praying the thump of her landing had gone unnoticed by the Minorcas. The house was very quiet. Perhaps they had gone to sleep.

River wasn't sure of the time, the sedative screwed up her time sense. Somehow everything had gone from daylight to night without her being aware of the change. One small lamp glowed in her bedroom and someone had dressed her in a soft white nightgown, a nightgown that was now bunched about her hips. She didn't waste much time wondering because there was something she was supposed to do. What was it? Her mind plodded across memory. This thing was of great importance to her, that much she remembered, but beyond that...well, it just wouldn't come.

Did it have something to do with the window? She lifted her eyes toward the elegantly draped aperture. A man had been there, she remembered that. A mocking man with fire.

Fire. Something to do with fire at the window.

She tried to lift her right hand and succeeded in slapping limply at her mouth. This incompetence was so frustrating.

Her dulled eyes swept to the wooden bedroom door and she idly wondered where it led. The door drew her and she made a few feeble attempts to crawl toward it before her attention was again pulled toward the window. Judging distances that seemed to change before her eyes, she eventually determined the window was closer than the door and she began to pull herself along the rug beneath her. After what seemed like hours, her hand closed on soft, heavy fabric. Cool, thin cotton brushed against her face and she giggled as it tickled her lips. Pressing these lips together, she nuzzled her nose against the sheer material.

Her fingers fumbled against something hard and she looked down at the floor. Someone had left a folded book of matches beneath the window. She tried to will her fingers to close on the matches and, after many attempts, managed to hold the small object between her forefinger and thumb. Fascinated, she studied it for some time, trying to remember how matches worked.

And then it came to her. She needed to light one of the matches to see Larken again.

Larken. River's mind wandered pleasantly as she remembered how Larken's hands felt on her body, how Larken's lips were so soft and firm, all at the same time. She remembered the smell of Larken's dark, heavy hair, the scent reminiscent of the goldenrod honey her father was so fond of back home in Virginia.

She saw Larken's wide, white smile, the laughter in her calm green eyes, the way her head tilted during lovemaking. She remembered their disagreements and how Larken's face could change from laughter to anger within seconds. She remembered

Larken's force, her strength, hands strong as she pressed her hard body to River's, and how her kicks and blows could cause dust to fly from the exercise bags. And then she saw Larken's *t'ai chi* and she wanted to weep anew at the beauty of her form.

Yes, she wanted to see Larken again, very much.

She looked at her hands and pulled her body into something resembling a sitting position. She fumbled the book of matches open and with much concentration, much effort, finally succeeded in pulling one of the paper matches loose from its fellows. She positioned the match just so in her fingers, her dry, thick tongue clasped between her lips and her eyes wide from the effort. She let her hand fall then, scraping the match along the black strip on the bottom of the book of matches. It didn't connect properly and no flame bloomed.

Disgusted, River flopped back to lie supine on the floor, her arms out to her sides, the book of matches in one hand, the lone match in the other. Sometime later, she lifted her arms and brought the two hands together.

CHAPTER FORTY-NINE

Larken couldn't wait any longer. She'd lost sight of Johosh in the binoculars and impatience seized her. Warily, she crept along the ground, her arms and hands suffering cuts from sharp grasses and lumps of coral. Approaching the house, she made a mental note of where each sentinel stood and the paths of the mobile guards.

One man sat alone, on a tree stump, not more than twenty-five feet from where Larken could emerge into the open area behind the house. She crept forward, stopping every few feet to ensure any sound she made would be dismissed as a normal sound of nature. Soon she was in the shadows, no more than five feet from the man.

He sat hunched forward, as if examining his hands. He moved every now and again, adjusting his suit coat, brushing dust from his polished shoes. Then he would hunch over again; it appeared as though he might be drowsing the time away.

Moving forward from the shadows, Larken was upon him in an instant, her fist crashing with controlled force into his spine, just below his head. Stunned, the nerves in the back of his neck shut his system down immediately and he fell over into a stupor.

Larken moved on.

The next guard was again on the perimeter of the grounds, standing alongside the driveway. A swift side kick to the solar plexus and an uppercut to the chin downed him.

She made her way toward a side door that had originally seemed less guarded than the other doors. Unfortunately, two men were standing there, conversing in low tones. Creeping up between them, she debated what to do. The voice of her old master and teacher, Huang Ko, rang in her mind. Do what must be done, he whispered.

Mouthing a silent chant of regret, she rushed forward and chopped outward with each of her strong hands, hitting each man below the Adam's apple and temporarily shutting off their air. Both men crumpled silently to the ground and Larken flattened herself against the door. Watching carefully to make sure no one observed, she turned the knob and slowly pushed inward.

The door led into a small anteroom, just off the laundry room. The sweet smell of laundry detergent and fabric softener almost made Larken sneeze but she managed to control the urge. Slipping inside, she closed the door, her heart leaping when the latch engaged with a small click. Silence returned as she stood motionless. Moving to the next inner door, Larken heard voices on the other side; servants, by their Cuban tongue. Would they sound an alarm? Warily, Larken pulled the door toward her and peered through the narrow opening. A group of women stood around a table. Though it was the wee hours of the morning they were packing suitcases with clothes folded neatly on the table. Two of the women were unpacking store boxes and Larken realized these were new clothes for a woman. Her jaw tightened. Had Simon bought these for River?

Larken's breathing increased as old fears resurfaced. Did River want to be here with him? Was Larken intruding? She reminded herself that these thoughts would be counterproductive to the task at hand and pushed them away, focusing on locating River. The rest could be dealt with later.

She realized suddenly that she smelled smoke and just as the information registered, a cry of fire sounded from upstairs. The women clustered frantically, babbling all the while, then hurried from the room.

Larken stepped through the door.

River watched the flame grow above her and finally realized that lighting the match could harm her. The hand holding the burning match dropped to one side and fell into a mass of paper wadded beneath the drapery. Fire grew in an instant and heat engulfed her.

Her mind leapt and she knew she needed to move back, to move away from that heat. Wearily, she turned her body and began the labor of pulling herself along the floor. As she turned however, her billowing gown touched the flame and, as if angered, the flame came after her. Itchy heat crept along her leg, finally searing, the pain causing adrenaline to flood her system.

She was going to die. It was unfair; she'd lit the flame just to see Larken and now she was going to die, not see the woman she loved, after all. She screamed, unsure whether it was from the scorching pain encompassing her leg or whether from the unfairness of not being able to be with Larken again.

CHAPTER FIFTY

Larken's soul withered at the sound of River's scream and she mounted the stairs three at a time. A disheveled Simon Minorca stood at the top of the stairs, sleepily looking about with blinking eyes. He saw Larken and his eyes widened.

"You! What are you doing here?"

"Get out of my way, Minorca," Larken growled, her teeth clamped together.

"Simon! It's in River's room," cried Minorca's mother from the upstairs hallway. "Come quickly!"

Minorca turned and moved along the hallway away from Larken. "Get away from there, Mother. It's not safe!"

The house, ancient by Key West standards, and constructed mostly of wood dried by years of sunlight and wind, grasped eagerly at the flame. Soon the entire front of the house was a sheet of crackling fire.

Larken fled along the hallway, bodily knocking Minorca and his mother to one side. She grasped the doorknob to the room nearest Patrice and immediately jerked her hand back due to the extreme heat. Grasping the hem of her T-shirt and using it to protect her hand, she turned the knob. Smoke and flame billowed out with frantic eagerness and she raised her arm to shield her face.

"River! Answer me! Where are you?"

She stumbled blind into the room and tripped over a form lying prone on the floor just inside.

"Oh, God," Larken moaned, bending to lift the body. River's gown was blackened and smoking, her platinum hair singed and gnarled by heat, her delicate skin blistered. Larken wasn't sure whether she was dead or alive but rushed from the room and down the burning hallway, River hanging limp in her arms. Larken didn't see the Minorcas as she fled along the stairway, lungs aching from the gray-black smoke roiling in all the fire-shrouded openings. Floating cinders burned her eyes and skin. A wall of fire met her at the bottom of the steps and she paused in indecision. Miraculously, Johosh was there, his leathery hand reaching for her through the wall of fire. He pulled them to safety and then she was outside, the glow from the fire brightening the night. She took great gulps of fresh air and laid River down on a patch of open sand.

Johosh moved toward one of the guards, pushing away any of Minorca's men who made as if to stop him. He pulled loose the bewildered man's jacket and fetched his cell phone from an inside pocket. He dialed then spoke rapidly into it.

"River? Please, River, talk to me!" Larken smoothed River's ruined hair from her face and touched her pale cheeks. Getting no response, she leaned and placed her ear against River's chest. There was some movement, but the heartbeat was weak, very faint, and Larken was suddenly filled with the fear of loss. She lifted River's limp form and sitting tailor-style, cradled her close. She rocked back and forth, crooning inanities as the house burned behind her.

CHAPTER FIFTY-ONE

Simon had lost all sense of direction. Holding his mother's hand, he tried to discern his way through the engulfing inferno growing all around them. Thick smoke obscured his vision, making progress slow, if not impossible. After moving away from the stairway, Simon had no idea which room they occupied, whether they had gone left into the living room or right into the foyer and dining room.

"Come this way!" his mother shrieked after many moments of indecision, tugging on his hand. She pulled him along, both stumbling over furniture, fiery boards raining down on their heads. Pushing against a swinging door, they entered the small closed area of the kitchen. Even here, the smoke was thick and full of burning cinders, choking them further. Simon tripped across something and fell to the cool tile floor. He gasped seeking air, as his mother fell on top of him, and that was how a new blast of fire and smoke found them a few seconds later. By the time the fire crew kicked in the back door, hoses at the ready, it was too late.

CHAPTER FIFTY-TWO

Outside the second-story apartment on Greene Street, strong sunlight frolicked with white-tipped ocean waves while chattering gulls danced on high thermals.

River turned away from the energizing scene and once again studied her face in a mirror hanging on the wall above a small vanity table. The burn on her cheek was no more than a slight abrasion now, though the more serious burns on her leg would be healing for quite some time. The pain wasn't much now, only troubling her when she exerted herself on her daily walks or let sunlight touch the bandages for too long.

Her eyes though. She wondered when the dullness left by the poison Simon had given her would fade away. Smiles were precious these days and her entire system felt sluggish and numb. River longed to run again, to freely laugh again.

"I just can't get used to you like that," Larken said, coming up behind River and studying their reflection in the mirror. She placed a darkly tanned hand on each side of River's neck and allowed long fingers to caress the soft wispy edges of her hair.

River sighed and studied her new razor-cut with equanimity. She'd never had her hair this short before but was growing to like it more each day. The short blond strands cradled her skull, almost like a halo. She smiled at her thoughts. A halo.

"That's what I like to see," said Larken with a grin. Kneeling, she placed her dark head next to River's, enjoying the contrast in the mirror.

"I love you, you know," she said quietly.

River turned her head and pressed her lips to Larken's cheek. "I love you, too."

Larken looked into River's eyes via the mirror. "So, no doubts?"

River returned the gaze, love replacing the somber cast of her eyes. "No, no doubts."

She paused then spoke again. "I still can't believe you thought I was his mistress."

"Well, I..."

River placed two fingers against Larken's lips. "Any doubts?"

"Naaah!" Larken replied with exaggerated nonchalance.

River giggled. "And you're sure of this?"

"Weren't you there last night? Didn't you see the erotic energy that transpired in that there bed?" She pointed off to one side, toward the big double bed, and River blushed.

Larken laughed and pulled River even closer. "I'm sorry, I didn't mean to embarrass you. I just wanted to let you know I feel completely loved and secure."

"Good!" River said emphatically. "There shouldn't be any question between us."

"Quite right," her lover agreed. "Although I do have one question."

River waited expectantly.

"Can people really make love like that when they've only

been out of the hospital two days? Shouldn't you be, like, in the *Guinness Book of World Records* or something?"

"That's two questions," River said, lifting her nose. "Now get out of my way. If we don't get going within the next few minutes, I'll miss saying goodbye to Mom and the others before they get on the plane."

"I like your family," Larken said, continuing to kneel in front of River.

"And they like you. A lot." She studied Larken then spoke teasingly. "I'm not sure why."

Larken grunted. "They're just glad you found someone who can tolerate you. Maybe take you off their hands."

River gave a push and Larken fell back playfully onto the wooden floorboards.

"You wench," Larken cried, "don't you realize I am now your boss?"

River laughed and shook her head. "I still can't believe Deidre really left it all to you. Simon would have been so pissed."

"I know," Larken agreed. "It's his own fault. He never got around to signing a partnership agreement so legally he had no rights at all. It was still her business completely. Not to speak harshly of the dead, but I really would have liked to have seen his face when I reminded him of that fact." She sighed and grinned at River.

"Yes, I know," River said, rolling her eyes. "I've only heard you talk about it, like, one hundred times..."

"Yep, so now, as my employee..." Larken's next words faded slowly away.

River had risen to her feet and limped to Larken's wardrobe to pull out a pair of shorts and a T-shirt. Watching Larken with teasing glances, she allowed her towel to drop, baring her delicious bottom and back to Larken's gaze.

"You wouldn't fire little old me now, would you?" she asked coyly, looking over her shoulder.

"Oh, man, you are wicked," Larken muttered, hiding her face with both hands.

She regained her feet with graceful ease and embraced River, turning her body in her arms. Her lips descended and

River was captured, knees weakening under the spell of Larken's kiss.

"Oh, what you do to me," Larken said some time later, pressing her chin to River's forehead.

With haste, she began stuffing River into her T-shirt, her fingers dragging only once across the swell of her breasts. She turned away and fetched panties from a drawer and slid them up River's sleek legs, carefully making sure they didn't catch on the large white bandage. Her cheek sought the smoothness of River's thigh and a gasp sounded above her. Larken jerked back and drew the light shorts up River's legs, diligently making sure the elasticized waistband was flattened and straight.

When she stepped away, River noticed the look of steely determination on Larken's face and a small laugh escaped her. "Good control, boss."

Larken agreed and turned away to run a brush through her thick mane. "Okay, I'm ready."

River had to laugh. Larken's ways were so simple and straightforward and her love so no-nonsense. River realized again how fortunate she was to have someone like Larken in her life.

"Hold me, Larken," she whispered.

Larken complied and they stood close for some time, a gentle, loving peace settling around them. River opened her eyes and caught a glimpse of herself in the vanity mirror. Her eyes were once again clear blue and sparkling.

She smiled at herself.

Publications from
Bella Books, Inc.
Women. Books. Even Better Together.
P.O. Box 10543
Tallahassee, FL 32302
Phone: 800-729-4992
www.bellabooks.com

CALM BEFORE THE STORM by Peggy J. Herring. Colonel Marcel Robicheaux doesn't tell and so far no one official has asked, but the amorous pursuit by Jordan McGowan has her worried for both her career and her honor.
978-0-9677753-1-9

THE WILD ONE by Lyn Denison. Rachel Weston is busy keeping home and head together after the death of her husband. Her kids need her and what she doesn't need is the confusion that Quinn Farrelly creates in her body and heart.
978-0-9677753-4-0

LESSONS IN MURDER by Claire McNab. There's a corpse in the school with a neat hole in the head and a Black & Decker drill alongside. Which teacher should Inspector Carol Ashton suspect? Unfortunately, the alluring Sybil Quade is at the top of the list. First in this highly lauded series.
978-1-931513-65-4

WHEN AN ECHO RETURNS by Linda Kay Silva. The bayou where Echo Branson found her sanity has been swept clean by a hurricane — or at least they thought. Then an evil washed up by the storm comes looking for them all, one-by-one. Second in series.
978-1-59493-225-0

DEADLY INTERSECTIONS by Ann Roberts. Everyone is lying, including her own father and her girlfriend. Leaving matters to the professionals is supposed to be easier! Third in series with *PAID IN FULL* and *WHITE OFFERINGS*.
978-1-59493-224-3

SUBSTITUTE FOR LOVE by Karin Kallmaker. No substitutes, ever again! But then Holly's heart, body and soul are captured by Reyna... Reyna with no last name and a secret life that hides a terrible bargain, one written in family blood.
978-1-931513-62-3

MAKING UP FOR LOST TIME by Karin Kallmaker. Take one Next Home Network Star and add one Little White Lie to equal mayhem in little Mendocino and a recipe for sizzling romance. This lighthearted, steamy story is a feast for the senses in a kitchen that is way too hot.
978-1-931513-61-6

2ND FIDDLE by Kate Calloway. Cassidy James's first case left her with a broken heart. At least this new case is fighting the good fight, and she can throw all her passion and energy into it.
978-1-59493-200-7

HUNTING THE WITCH by Ellen Hart. The woman she loves — used to love — offers her help, and Jane Lawless finds it hard to say no. She needs TLC for recent injuries and who better than a doctor? But Julia's jittery demeanor awakens Jane's curiosity. And Jane has never been able to resist a mystery. #9 in series and Lammy-winner.
978-1-59493-206-9

FAÇADES by Alex Marcoux. Everything Anastasia ever wanted — she has it. Sidney is the woman who helped her get it. But keeping it will require a price — the unnamed passion that simmers between them.
978-1-59493-239-7

ELENA UNDONE by Nicole Conn. The risks. The passion. The devastating choices. The ultimate rewards. Nicole Conn rocked the lesbian cinema world with Claire of the Moon and has rocked it again with Elena Undone. This is the book that tells it all...
978-1-59493-254-0

WHISPERS IN THE WIND by Frankie J. Jones. It began as a camping trip, then a simple hike. Dixon Hayes and Elizabeth Colter uncover an intriguing cave on their hike, changing their world, perhaps irrevocably.
978-1-59493-037-9

WEDDING BELL BLUES by Julia Watts. She'll do anything to save what's left of her family. Anything. It didn't seem like a bad plan...at first. Hailed by readers as Lammy-winner Julia Watts' funniest novel.
978-1-59493-199-4

WILDFIRE by Lynn James. From the moment botanist Devon McKinney meets ranger Elaine Thomas the chemistry is undeniable. Sharing — and protecting — a mountain for the length of their short assignments leads to unexpected passion in this sizzling romance by newcomer Lynn James.
978-1-59493-191-8

LEAVING L.A. by Kate Christie. Eleanor Chapin is on the way to the rest of her life when Tessa Flanaghan offers her a lucrative summer job caring for Tessa's daughter Laya. It's only temporary and everyone expects Eleanor to be leaving L.A...
978-1-59493-221-2

SOMETHING TO BELIEVE by Robbi McCoy. When Lauren and Cassie meet on a once-in-a-lifetime river journey through China their feelings are innocent...at first. Ten years later, nothing — and everything — has changed. From Golden Crown winner Robbi McCoy.
978-1-59493-214-4

DEVIL'S ROCK: THE SEARCH FOR PATRICK DOE by Gerri Hill. Deputy Andrea Sullivan and Agent Cameron Ross vow to bring a killer to justice. The killer has other plans. Gerri Hill pens another intriguing blend of mystery and romance in this page-turning thriller.
978-1-59493-218-2

SHADOW POINT by Amy Briant. Madison Maguire has just been not-quite fired, told her brother is dead and discovered she has to pick up a five-year old niece she's never met. After she makes it to Shadow Point it seems like someone—or something—doesn't want her to leave. Romance sizzles in this ghost story from Amy Briant.
978-1-59493-216-8

JUKEBOX by Gina Daggett. Debutantes in love. With each other. Two young women chafe at the constraints of parents and society with a friendship that could be more, if they can break free. Gina Daggett is best known as "Lipstick" of the columnist duo Lipstick & Dipstick.
978-1-59493-212-0

BLIND BET by Tracey Richardson. The stakes are high when Ellen Turcotte and Courtney Langford meet at the blackjack tables. Lady Luck has been smiling on Courtney but Ellen is a wild card she may not be able to handle.
978-1-59493-211-3